Sky Breaking 301
Hellkitten Chronicles Book 3

By

Viola Grace

Sky Breaking seemed like a useful course, but its usefulness lay in the amount of credits that would count toward Imara's degree.

Once she is in the course, she meets the only other student, and they strike an unlikely friendship. Kitigan is a seer who has an interest in farming and apiculture, weather magic is part of that peculiar parcel.

After a series of classes that turn into tests, Imara is happy to head to Kitty's farm for a weekend away from school, and Mr. E wants to head out and ride some sheep. Everybody has something to do, including the trespassing werewolf pack that just moved in next to Kitty's family farm.

Imara has to walk the fine line between guest and defender while taking her Death Keeper skills for a spin. Her weekend is anything but relaxing.

The characters and events in this book are fictitious. Any similarity to real persons, living or dead, is coincidental and not intended by the author.

Look for me online at violagrace.com, Sea to Sky Books, Amazon, Smashwords, Kobo, B&N and other eBook sellers.

Chapter One

Smara was curled up on the couch, doing some advanced reading for her next round of courses when Reegar wandered by. "So, your familiar is taking up hobbies?"

She blinked and stared at the spectre. "Yeah, he said he wanted to do something with his spare time. Why?"

"I had to help him with the welding tank. His paws couldn't turn the—"

She was up and out of her chair, heading down the hall with all the speed she could muster. When she got to the lab, she grabbed the frame and whipped around the corner.

She took in Mr. E in his safety gear

and the objects he was welding together. It seemed better to wait until his foot was off the pedal that was controlling the gas before she spoke with him. "Mr. E, what are you doing?"

He was in prairie dog position, and as she asked, he pushed his goggles up to look at her with his adorable kittenish eyes. *I admired blacksmiths while I was a child, now that you have indicated I could entertain myself while you were studying, I decided to take up the hobby. It is more difficult with fur and my paws, but Reegar is helpful if bizarrely amused.*

Imara pinched the bridge of her nose. "I think he is wondering where you got the goggles."

Mr. E lashed his tail. *Bara obtained it for me, once Reegar explained what I needed.*

"Ah. Well, what are you making?"

He moved his small black body between her and his project. *I am just ex-perimenting right now. I will let you know when I have something worth observing.*

"So, you want me to go?"

Please. You may call upon me if you need me, but I believe you are doing fine with your studies.

"So, you are telling me to bug off."

I would never do that, my dear mage-in-training. But I enjoy the thought of making something with my own paws and minimal magic.

"If you get sparked, let me know. I will come running."

He let out a small purr, and his chin lifted. *Thank you. Enjoy your studies.*

She inclined her head and backed out the door, waiting until she heard him start up again before she snuck her phone around the corner and took a picture of her kitten with a blowtorch.

Chuckling, she glanced at the image

for the next two hours while she went over the basics of weather manipulation.

Imara was sitting and studying when Bara burst in, "Imara, turn on the TV. Argus is on the news."

Imara closed her book and sat up, grabbing the remote and turning on the television. Bara grabbed the remote and flicked to a local station.

"Where are they?" Imara was watching footage from the previous night.

"There was a riot around Ritual Space. They have started to restrict bookings, and some wizard groups are complaining." Bara sat next to her on the couch.

They watched the XIA team round up the wizards who were disturbingly naked. Imara tried not to look, but the festively decorated bodies were hypnotic.

Bara snorted. "They were one of those *male magic is stronger* groups. I guess they pissed off the proprietor."

Imara wrinkled her nose as the Mage Guild bus pulled up and the men were handed off to those who would be able to deal with them. Epithets were fired from the arrested men to the non-humans that had cuffed them, but Argus and his team kept their cool in front of the camera.

The reporter tried to get them to speak, but the door to the space opened, and they excused themselves as the guild vehicle hauled the idiots off for processing.

The reporter smiled tightly and signed off.

Bara snickered and turned the television off. "Just thought you would like to at least see him this week. You two sure have an odd relationship."

Imara sighed and drummed her fingers on her book. "We are doing just fine. I am on a fast track through school, and he is dealing with whatever happens on his shifts. We connect when we can.”

“From what I can see, you two don’t *connect* at all.” Bara looked idly down at her fingernails.

“None of your business, but I am a little young for him, according to him. I also have a business plan that we both want to see put into action. There is plenty of time for connections after that.”

Bara sighed and leaned against the back of the couch. “You are so serious.”

“That is my lot in life. On the other side, I am smarter than heck, have a few good friends, and a weirdly determined familiar, so I am feeling pretty good about myself.” Imara opened her book and found her page. The smug smirk on her lips probably didn’t become her, but she was enjoying the feeling of security that her surroundings were giving her.

A thought occurred to her. “By the

way, how did Mr. E ask you for the goggles?"

Bara chuckled. "Reegar translated for him. Is he really using them?"

"Yeah. I think a welding shield would be better. He has a lot of fluff."

"Noted. I will keep an eye out. I am really enjoying the textile studies." Bara sighed happily.

Imara went back to her book, and Bara interrupted her again.

"Why are you studying across the board?"

Imara looked up and cocked her head. "How long have you wanted to ask?"

"Since last term."

Snickering, Imara tapped the book in her lap. "For what I want to do, a business course is basically what I need, but to get my certification and guild membership, I need my degree. Learning what I can about other aspects of magic and its application can only help me in the long run."

"So, you still want to be an investigator?"

Imara corrected her. "A spectral consultant. Outside of the Death Keepers, the spectres don't talk to anyone. They can't."

"So, since you are a registered Death Keeper..."

"Technically an apprentice, but I am part of the guild."

"So, you can go right from graduation to consultant with a degree to propel you into full Mage Guild status."

"That is the plan. In the meantime, I am taking advantage of the largest collection of instructors and specialists on the continent. I have half the business classes already taken care of and am looking forward to whisking through the next three terms."

Bara gave her a long look. "Aren't you

even tempted to delay just to experience college life?"

Imara shook her head. "Nope. I have been around enough partiers in my life to know that it might be interesting, but it leaves more regret than most folks want to admit. I would rather barrel through and save the regretful social situations for after I graduate."

"Are you planning on having any?"

Grinning, Imara turned back to her book. "I have every confidence in my ability to get into trouble, with or without my familiar."

"I have to say, I am glad to hear it. You are way too put together for someone your age. You make me look bad."

Imara found the spot where she had been reading about the effect of magic on thermal currents. "I don't. I just focus on my future. I have been planning it since I was four, so it is nice that I am finally here and my little self didn't know what a kegger was, so it wasn't in the plan."

Bara snorted and left her alone.

Imara got through two chapters before she felt a tingle and smelled scorched hair. She got up and had her glass in her hand the moment that Mr. E barrelled around the corner, the top of his head on fire.

She dumped the ice water on the flames and picked him up, removing his goggles and heading for the kitchen. A light tingle of magic ran through their connection, and she watched as the discoloured skin at the top of his head heal and then sprout fluffy fur.

He sighed and relaxed in her grip. *I didn't think I would catch fire.*

"That was silly of you. I am sorry, but you were designed to be a kitten, and kittens need to eat, sleep, and they are flammable."

He mumbled something about stupid

mages and cuddled into her arms. *My head is still wet.*

Imara sat and rubbed the growing fur slowly with a kitchen towel.

The spectre of Magus Reegar materialized in the kitchen. "Was he on fire? There is a trail of singed hair from the lab to the entertainment room."

She smiled as Mr. E gave Reegar a narrow-eyed look. "He was. I don't know if he is finished with his project."

Reegar nodded. "I will turn off the equipment."

He disappeared, and Imara continued to soothe her grumpy familiar.

In his previous life, he may have been a homicidal mage on a mission, but now, he was her kitten, and he needed attention. She scratched under his chin, and his little body started a heavy purr. Yeah, he was a terrifying monster. She was lucky to have him.

Don't forget it. He gave a delicate

yawn. *How are the weather magic studies coming?*

"They are fine. I think I am grasping the thermal drifts and how to use nature to magnify the effects."

Good. Prepare to be quizzed.

"What?"

In a volcanic habitat, how do you generate snow?

She blinked, and he made a mental ticking clock noise. Apparently, class was starting a few days early.

"You begin by locating a water source, and then, you check the temperature of the magma..." She continued to pet him as she worked her way through the options of the techniques she had just learned. It wasn't going to be the right answer, but it was an answer. That was a start.

Class was in session, and the professor was almost over his ouchie.

Chapter Two

Your suitor is definitely worthy of your attentions. The smug voice was laced with satisfaction from his position on his new perch.

Imara smiled and kept hiking. "I am glad you are enjoying it. I still have no idea what to get him for his birthday, whenever it is."

The new backpack was wide, sturdy, and had a shelf built into the top for Mr. E to park his fuzzy butt. She was his Sherpa through the campus, and he was enjoying the ride.

The summer session was in full swing, and the campus was nearly empty. Only the die-hard students were still attending. Half the faculty was on vacation.

The field she was walking through had a single pathway in it, and it was enough of a hint that she was in the right place that she didn't panic. The building that she was looking for had to be around here somewhere.

It is underground. Look for a large stone slab and stand on it for one minute. It will take you down. Mr. E seemed to have worn off his dizzy fun, and he was now taking her finding her course location seriously.

"How do you know that?"

I asked Reegar. He is a fountain of information. He shared a similar worldview to mine and is delighted to have me under his roof. I am one of his heroes.

"Oh, man. That isn't good."

I beg to differ. Despite my sentence, I had no idea that I had an underground cult following. It is heartening to hear that folks don't go for demonic intervention anymore.

"I don't think it was a trend that could have remained for any length of time."

It had begun to take on a cataclysmic pace. It had to be stopped, so I stopped it.

She wrinkled her nose. "And the guild obviously didn't disagree with your actions, or they would have sentenced you to death and not familial repayment."

Death would have been quick; this is an eternity of servitude. It is much worse.

"Thanks for that." She spotted the stone panel that he had described.

Imara, you are the bright spot in an otherwise tedious existence, even if your choice of forms for me could have been slightly more masculine.

She grinned and stepped in the centre

of the circular pad. A click was audible, and the pad she stood on slowly lowered into the earth.

Weather control was about to begin.

"You won't need your familiar. It can wait here." The woman who spoke was distinctively green.

Imara set her backpack down, got out Mr. E's food and water and turned back to her instructor. "There, he is all set."

The dryad nodded. "Good. Now, the other student is this way. You will be working as a team."

"Other student? I thought there would be more."

"This is an advanced class, Ms. Mirrin. Few could make it through the selection process."

The structure they were in was stone. The walls, floors, and archways that led into other parts of the underground warren were all stone.

"Am I late?"

"No, you are on time. I believe the other student forgot to set her clock, but the Deegles have always been funny about time."

"Do I need my books?"

"No. You can read the theory after the lessons. It will give you more reference points then, and you won't overthink it."

Imara blushed. She had read all the texts twice. Her brain was whirling with situations and adjustments. She just had to try to tamp down those impulses when it came time to actually working with magic.

They walked down a hall, and a huge amphitheatre waited for them. There was one small figure sitting in the first row with glints of light coming from her hands when she moved. She moved a lot.

The dryad nodded to the other woman. "Introduce yourselves. I will set up the first lab."

Imara walked up to the other student and sat next to her. "Hiya. I am Imara, and it looks like we are it in this class."

The woman looked at her and nodded, her clothing dotted by orbs dangling from nearly every available surface. The woman smiled and extended her hand, covered in rings with small orbs on them. "I am Kitigan, but most folks call me Kitty."

Imara shook her hand in greeting and enjoyed the amused twinkle in the other young woman's eyes. "Pleased to meet you."

"You as well. I have heard interesting things about you." She quirked her lips.

"Nothing bad."

"Nope. I took a course on bookkeeping with one of your brother's last term. During a study group, he mentioned that you had joined the school."

Their instructor finished organizing

herself and tapped her lectern. "Okay, ladies. Pleasantries are over. I am Weather Witch Annamaria Eckoak. You may address me as Eckoak. Yes, I am a dryad, but my father was a weather wizard, and it is a family skill. I am here to try and transfer natural talent into deliberate action. Sky breaking is a difficult skill to learn."

Kitty cleared her throat. "Sky breaking?"

Eckoak inclined her head and raised her hand. As she spoke, a cloud formed ten inches over her palm. "You are taking air, wind, water, heat, radiation, and anything else in the vicinity and inserting it into the existing weather pattern to assert your will. You are breaking the pattern and making another. You have to see where it is going and where it will end. The most important thing is to contain it. Now, I want each of you to come up here and try to replicate this particular effect. I want to see a storm in your palms."

Imara blinked. "What?"

"Storm in your hands, ladies. Now. Come here and give it a try." Eckoak gave them a slight and encouraging smile.

Imara walked to face her instructor with a dazed feeling. Her mind ran through all of the information she had absorbed over the last few days, and she held out her hands as Kitty joined her in front of the lectern.

She focused on finding water, but the air around her was dry. Deliberately, she didn't look at either of her companions as she spit into her palm to start things off.

Imara inhaled, exhaled, using her body as a heat source and her breath for wind. The tiny cloud began to form, and it flickered for a moment before dissipating and leaving her shaking and exhausted.

She dropped her hands to her sides and watched as Kitty cupped her hands together and blew softly. A tiny tornado formed, shooting upward before Kitty let it lose steam.

Eckoak looked up and made a *tsk* sound. "Sloppy but encouraging. Let me just grab that wind before it gets hostile."

Imara looked up, and against the stone ceiling was her little white puff of cloud colliding with the tiny tornado. Together, the systems connected and danced until they started to grow.

Their instructor extended her hands and beckoned. The weather system coiled downward until it rested in her palms. When she closed her fists, the issue was contained.

Imara blinked. "Wow. I thought I had let my weather system go."

Kitty nodded, sweat on her brow. "I

thought so, too."

"You did, but moving air never stops." Eckoak continued to compact her hands together until they were flat. "That is why we are learning underground. Down here, it can be contained, but out there, you could kill someone."

Kitty swayed, and Imara reached out to hold onto her. "Easy." If she was honest, she needed contact for support as well.

Eckoak's lips quirked slightly, the first true amusement she had shown. "Now, what did you do wrong, aside from enrolling in this course?"

Apparently, the class had begun, and Imara had faltered at the first test. It was not a great start.

Eckoak watched the two exhausted mages stumbling back toward the entrance after four hours of focus and concentration. Her smile bloomed the moment that they were out of sight.

She closed up the auditorium and took the administration exit to the chancellor's home. She walked up the path and knocked on the door. When her friend opened it, Eckoak smiled. "Tea. Now."

"It's ready. I even included sandwiches." Mirrin winked.

Eckoak followed her college friend into the sitting room, and she smiled in delight at the spread that Mirrin had created for her. "This won't get her a better grade."

Mirrin chuckled and settled in her seat, pouring tea for both of them. "She gets what she earns, Koki."

Eckoak smirked. "She will do fine. She is a reader, isn't she?"

"I have heard reports that she might be making her way through Reegar's library."

"That would explain it. She made a

pocket cloud on her first day."

Mirrin's hand shook when she handed over the cup and saucer. "She did?"

"Yes. She has focus and drive. Imagine what she could have done if she had been trained since childhood. It boggles the imagination."

Mirrin frowned. "She had a good education. My family saw to that."

"And yet, she was raised in a non-magical city barely touched by the Wave. It was sheer luck that she was offered the position of Death Keeper."

The chancellor shook her head. "It wasn't luck. My aunt is a Death Keeper, as are two of my siblings. They knew who they were taking on board."

"Well, well, well. Here I thought that you always played by the rules." Koki bit into the first sandwich. The thinly sliced salmon melted in her mouth.

"I did. None of us were in contact with her. My family simply looked out for its own and mentioned her aptitude to the right people at the proper time." The smile was that of the proud mother.

Koki sat back and sighed. "Well, she does have aptitude. Having read all of her files, she can do just about anything, so why is she trying to speed through college?"

"She has a plan, and she has a focus. If she wants to return to education later, I am all for it, but for now, she knows where she needs to be."

"How can you be sure? She's so young." Koki nibbled her way through another sandwich.

"She has nearly two decades of focus behind her. Personally, I think she came out of me knowing where she would end up. She had a career plan even then."

Koki laughed. "Did you regret being separated from her?"

"Every moment for the last two decades. I have kept my eye on her as best I could through family and guild connections, but the moment she got here, I nearly burst out of my skin." Mirrin grinned, "Reegar was a little put out at the beginning, but now, I think he actually looks on her as a niece of some sort."

"And now, you have roped me into the education of your offspring." Koki frowned.

"Hey, I made you tea, and those teeny sandwiches with the crusts cut off. You know how painful domestic stuff is for me."

"I accept that. The other student looks to be a good social match for her as well."

Mirrin held her hand up in surrender. "That was none of my doing. The Deegle girl is smart, and she has a lot of skills, but I have no idea what her personality is like. If she made it into the course and past your vetting, I am sure she is a worthy student."

"She is. If she and your daughter were one student, they would be exceptional. As it is, the two will manage to produce a decent storm by the end of the term, together or individually." The dryad watched her friend battle with pride and concern.

The seven sons that had applied to the weather magic course had yielded only two that she accepted. The daughter was almost made of different stuff. Imara was bright, cheerful, and determined. It was a change from the sullen entitlement of her brothers. Well, all of the brothers but the youngest, but he wasn't suited to weather work. There was too much fire in that boy.

"I have your room set up." Mirrin smiled as she refilled Koki's tea.

"So, the backyard, a tree, and the potting shed?"

"Yup."

Koki laughed and toasted her with the teacup. "Excellent. You are a sublime hostess for those in touch with the soil."

"Thank you. I do try. Do you think that Imara would mind me watching her lesson?"

Koki blinked. "I think she wouldn't even notice you were there. She has a brain for weather; she just needs to tune the rest of the world out. It will be difficult for her. She is desperate to move with the world around her."

"My fault. She needed more socialization. More friends."

"As you said, she made her choices. She is learning to live with them."

Mirrin looked out the front window and pursed her lips. "I want to help."

"Which shows that you are still her mother even if you couldn't raise her. Now, get over that and hand me another sandwich. If I have to teach your precious child tomorrow, I need some more sustenance." Koki smirked and watched as Mirrin went back to the kitchen for more food.

It took a lot to distract the chancellor, but Koki hoped that a small break from worry would be enough for her.

Imara needed more focus, and Mirrin needed less. Yeah, they definitely were related.

Chapter Three

The moment that Eckoak dismissed them, Imara retreated down the hall. Kitty walked in the same staggering steps that Imara figured she was using.

When they got to the entry vestibule, Imara collected Mr. E from the top of her backpack. He had slept the whole morning through.

"What are you doing next?" Kitty waited while Imara grabbed her stuff.

"I think lunch is in order. How about you?"

"The same. Did you want to go together?"

Imara blinked in surprise. "Sure. There is a nice diner a few blocks from here if you like."

Kitty beamed. "Great. I'll head up first and wait for you."

Imara chuckled and nodded, settling her familiar in the crook of her arm and her pack on her back.

Kitty headed up on the circular flagstone, and it returned to take Imara up in moments.

Out in the sudden warmth of the summer day, Imara swayed. Mr. E woke up with a yawn and a stretch.

You smell of sweat. It appears you got quite the workout.

"I did. Now, shush and get back on the pack."

He stretched and climbed her arm, settling in his little spot and curling up tight.

"You have a familiar?" Kitty was staring.

"I do. Apparently, he is an inherited familiar. Bloodlines and all that." She shrugged. "I honestly have no idea. I needed a familiar for one of my classes, and he is what I ended up with. His name is Mr. E."

Kitty laughed. "Such a formal name for a kitten. Why is he glaring at me?"

"He takes offense easily, but he is working on developing hobbies, so I have hope for his personal growth." Imara could feel his indignation in their connection. She reached over her shoulder and scratched his chin. The small, rumbling purr started immediately.

"I have a bunch of questions for you."

Imara nodded. "I have one or two for you as well, but we can talk over lunch. I am starving."

They started the walk to the diner, and Kitty chuckled. "If it is about the balls, they are a family magic."

"How does that work?"

"It is a little embarrassing, but I can see through time but only as long as the orb will let me. Once I use one, it is burned out until I can reset or replace it."

"So, you are covered with them..."

"So, if I need to, I can check my future five seconds at a time."

"Is that handy?"

Kitty wrinkled her nose. "Not particularly."

They laughed at complicated family magic and made their way to the diner.

As she looked at the menu, Imara asked, *Mr. E, did you want anything?*

He was seated next to her, still on the top of the backpack. He looked over her shoulder, and his tail started lashing. *I would like a banana cream pie.*

Slice?

No, the pie.

This I have got to see.

You are going to. Order me some napkins as well. This is going to get messy.

Imara wasn't sure, but she thought that Mr. E was rubbing his paws together.

She exhaled and looked at her own selection. Cheeseburger with bacon and fries. Yup. She was playing to the old standards, but as a back-to-school food, it couldn't be beaten.

Kitty was biting her lip and glancing at Imara. "Do you know what you are ordering?"

"I do. You?"

"I can't decide. You go first."

When the server arrived, she cooed over Mr. E, who preened himself and let out a small *mew*.

Imara rolled her eyes and ordered. "Cheeseburger with bacon, fries, side salad, and a banana cream pie."

The server blinked. "A slice?"

"No, the whole pie, please. My familiar is a glutton."

Mr. E washed his little paw daintily in

preparation for his food orgy.

Kitty cleared her throat and ordered a hamburger with a side of potato salad.

When the server was gone, Kitty gave Imara a thankful look. "I was terrified you would be a vegetarian."

Imara was flabbergasted. "Why?"

"I don't know. A lot of the women I have met here have been vegetarians, and I thought you might be one of them."

"I like how you describe them as a different species."

Kitty grinned, "They feel like that sometimes. My sister went veggie for a while. She was intolerable. My mom almost strangled her when she tried to liberate the livestock."

"Livestock?"

Her new companion blushed. "Yeah, I am from a farming family."

"What kind of animals?"

"You are genuinely interested?"

That was surprising. "Of course. I am new to this entire setting. I have been working to get through school my whole life, and it leaves very little exposure to other family styles or environments."

"Dairy and wool. Cows and sheep. Normally, they don't get along, but Mom's family were dairy farmers, and Dad's were shepherds. They consolidated, and now, we have a few hundred acres of useful animals."

"Which part of your family uses the orbs?"

Kitty leaned back as the server brought their drinks. "My dad's. He is also a glassmaker, and he makes the spheres for me."

"Not for himself?"

She rolled her eyes. "No. Since I was going away to school, he wanted me prepared to see my future at any interval. With the stuff I am wearing, I could probably get through a few months if I had to."

"Why so many?" Imara sipped at her water.

"Dads." Kitty shrugged as if Imara should understand.

She should understand, but there was no way she ever would. It was her father that had rejected her as a member of his brood, and it wasn't something that she could just give to the universe. Forgive and forget was difficult when she hadn't even been able to meet most of her relatives.

"Before you ask, I don't use them to cheat on exams."

Imara laughed. "I never thought you would. The instructors know about it, and most of the exams are practical. There is no advantage to knowing the future when you are just going to have to go through with it anyway."

Kitty looked at her with a stunned smile on her lips. "Exactly."

The food arrived, and when the pie was set on the table, Mr. E jumped right in. The cute noises he was making did not deter from the orgy of consumption he was engaged in.

Imara put some more ketchup on her burger and on her fries, picked up her food, and dug in. She had seen his cute feeding frenzy before.

Kitty grabbed her burger and dug in. They ate in silence as the tiny cat stomped and munched his way through the pie.

A few people stopped by their table and took recordings of Mr. E wearing the pie before he ate it, but when Imara was done, Mr. E finished and worked at cleaning himself completely.

Kitty was halfway through her potato salad when Imara began to help Mr. E clean himself up.

"He ate all of it?"

"He did, but he hates getting wet, so I

am going to dry towel him, and he can finish his grooming after that."

"How could it fit?" Kitty seemed genuinely astonished.

"Um, he isn't an actual kitten. He is an energy being in a kitten shell. He can eat as much as he wants." Imara finished wiping the cream off his paws, and he settled back against the sugar dispenser to suck his toes clean.

"But... he looks like a kitten."

"Yes, and he is supposed to, but he isn't. He is much more intelligent and devious than your average kitten. Also, slightly more homicidal."

Mr. E yawned and blinked at Kitty with wide green eyes. He was really putting on the cute.

"I don't think he is dangerous."

Imara remembered the sight of him transforming and attacking her enemy. "Yeah, you can think that, but wait until you have a snack that he wants."

Kitty chuckled and continued to eat.

Sitting back, Imara asked, "Why are you taking the weather magic course?"

"Farming folk. If I can create a separate weather system over the fields for just a day or even a few hours, it would make all the difference. You?"

"It is three credits toward my graduation and one of the only courses running over the summer term that I qualify for. I also thought it would look good toward guild membership."

Kitty nodded. "Makes sense. Have you tried to add a few community factors? I mean, if you are going for rapid guild membership, volunteering is an excellent way to get a leg up."

"Volunteering? Where?"

"The student office should have some information for you, but I volunteer to take the Mage Guides around the farm and introduce them to the animals."

"Are you a Guide?" In her circles, the

thought of having a childhood organization that would assist with magical development was nearly mythical.

"I was. Now, I just volunteer. You never joined?"

Imara wrinkled her nose. "I was in a non-magical city. No Guides. We knew about them, but we didn't have them."

"Do you have a skill that you could teach eager little girls? If you do, I can help you get in touch with a local chapter."

Imara's growing hope fell. "Nope, nothing special."

Mr. E loudly rattled the sugar container. *Death Keeping is not common. I think they would enjoy meeting spectres.*

Did you have the Mage Guides and Scouts when you were young?

No, but we did have schools that scouted for children with magical skills. They were brought in whether their families were in favour of it or not. He was being a very grim kitten.

Kitty pushed her empty plate aside. "You are talking to him?"

"I was. He reminded me that I am an apprentice Death Keeper. I could take the girls on a tour of the mage repositories if there are any around here."

"A Death Keeper? Seriously? Oh, man. None of the ones in this area have been willing to talk to the Guides. They say that young girls don't respect the seriousness of the situation."

Imara snorted. "Of course, they don't, but once they meet one of their ancestors, they usually smarten up."

Kitty was stunned. "You can do that?"

A blush started on her cheeks. "Oh, yeah. I have an affinity for death. I can have a conversation with most mages after they have passed. I mean, if they were properly laid to rest and their spectre released."

Kitty rubbed her hands together and grinned. "You are going to be very popular."

"I believe I am regretting mentioning it." Her palms were sweating.

"Don't worry. If you can get access, I can get you a volunteering credit." There was complete confidence in her tone.

"I will believe it when I see it. Now, how did you manage to make that tornado today?" Her change of topic wasn't subtle, but it was effective. They delved into the different techniques that they had used, and each learned a little something from the other. If it weren't for Mr. E snoring like a lumberjack, it would have been a really good study session. Laughter tended to break the flow of thought.

Chapter Four

"You want to what?" The voice on the other end of the line was shocked.

"I want to bring a group of Mage Guides to the repository after sundown so that they can speak with an actual spectre. It is an important step in their joining the magical community and not something that can be offered by someone who is not a Death Keeper."

"There is no availability for a staff member to take them on a *tour* of the dead."

"There doesn't have to be. I am a Death Keeper Guild member, and I can keep less than a dozen girls from running amok in a graveyard." She crossed her fingers.

"Give me your credentials, and I will get back to you if we have an evening available if I believe you can manage the visit. Don't hold your breath."

"Right. Apprentice Imara Mirrin of Sakenta. My number is—"

"I have it. Have a pleasant evening."

She winced as the click sounded in her ear, but it was hopeful. Thomins would give her a good reference, she was sure of it. She just needed to live up to her promise to keep control of the Guides. From what the Guide Master had said, they would be a handful.

He was rude. Mr. E was sitting on her desk and supervising her studies. He had jostled her into making the call, and now, he had the nerve to make a critique.

"He was a Death Keeper. They rarely work with the living. He will call back. Thomins said I was a natural and he would miss me when I left."

Did he want to sleep with you?

"Uh, no. When I started there, I was still a child. If he did, he would be a pervert, and I never got that vibe from him."

Hmph. Well, I still think that the idiot on the phone was ru—

The phone rang, the cheerful tune belted out of the slick rectangle, and after checking the number, Imara answered it.

"Hello?"

"Apprentice Mirrin, I apologize. Of course, we would be happy to have your group of *girls* come for a visit. Will you be waking the spectres?"

Imara grinned. "Yes. If you have any of their families or custodians who wish a consultation, I will bring a little more stability to some of the ones who are fading."

"Excellent! Yes, I will. Do you need

anything?"

"Yes, please find a spectre who would be willing to answer questions about their situation. I would like to impress upon them that death is not the end. They will leave their knowledge behind."

There was a pause. "Right. That is... you have summed it up nicely."

"That was my job. I met with the families and took them to their spectres. I had to make it seem pleasant, and these girls will be introduced to it as gently as I can make it. May I have a date?"

"Name your day, and we will accommodate you."

"I will contact the Guide Master and call you back. Thank you so much. The girls will be on their best behaviour."

A few more pleasantries and they ended the call.

The next call was to the Guide Master, and the woman was so enthusiastic, she promised to get back to Imara within the hour when she had all of the agreements from the Guides' parents.

Imara exhaled and looked at her phone as if it was a snake. "Well, Kitty was definitely right. There is a demand for Death Keepers in the area."

There is a demand for you. You know that your skills with the energies of the dead are not normal, right?

She wrinkled her nose and scratched Mr. E behind his ear until he let out a purr that rattled his little body. "I have suspected as much for quite a while. Now, quiz me on the types of clouds. We are having a test next week, and I want to be ready."

Shouldn't you be studying with Kitty? He narrowed his eyes as if he knew what she was going to say.

"I *am* studying with a kitty. No, she is busy with her apiary course. Bees are bees."

Two weeks after their first class, Imara was pretty sure that she had made another friend. Kitty had a great sense of humour, and despite her accessories, she was bright and had skills when it came to shifting weather.

Too bad. You need practice on your heat control.

"We are doing a lab tomorrow. The workspace is open, and we can let loose a little."

It was confining to have to wait until they had lab time in the underground complex, but it was probably for the best as neither of them was particularly skilled at taking their creations apart once they had gotten them going. There weren't a lot of places to hide in the lecture hall, but they had found most of them.

After a few minutes of studying, she looked at her phone and smiled.

It is the courtier, is it?

"Of course. It is our normal check-in

time. He has had a good start to his night, and I am just about ready to pass out. It is the best time for a little technological contact.”

The snort that came from Mr. E should not have been possible for such a small body. *I find it hard to believe that you are content to be distant from him. I can feel everything that runs through you when he is near. It is enough to make me blush.*

“You keep your assessments to yourself. We are waiting for any of that stuff. It would be too distracting if I threw myself into a physical relationship before my studies are done. I don’t want to chance a pregnancy before I get what I want.”

I thought that modern technology fixed all that.”

She huffed and gave him a dark look. “Magic gets around that sort of thing, as you well know.”

It has never been a concern of mine. My family was banished during my sentencing. The line died out during my fourth term as familiar.

"Oh, geez. I am so sorry, Mr. E. I had no idea."

He shrugged and curled himself into a small ball. *No reason you should have.*

The silence between them was heavy, so she closed her books, scooped him up, and carried him to her bed where she sat and stroked his ears until his body relaxed. No matter what the situation was, family wasn't easy.

"Ladies, today we are working on lightning." Eckoak was sitting on top of the lectern with a jaunty grin.

Mr. E was out in the vestibule with a book on metallurgy, so Imara didn't worry about what they were about to do.

Kitty gave her a worried look. "I am not sure about this."

Eckoak chuckled. "No one ever is. The bright spark is the first visible crackle of power for most elementals. Neither of you are elementals, so this is not going to be fun. I have heard that it hurts the first time."

Kitty snorted until she realized that their instructor was serious.

Imara nodded. "Right. How do we start?"

Eckoak smiled. "That is the spirit. Now, go and stand on those thick rubber mats."

Imara headed to the first of the mats, and she dried her hands on her jeans. This was not the moment to have any water involved.

At the far end of the chamber, a cage was wheeled out, pushed by a man with seriously messed up hair and a chalky complexion.

"Who is he?" Kitty asked it before Imara could.

"Tellfirth works with the Mage Guild when they send their officers on assignment. He's a medic. If you accidentally stop your own hearts, he can get you started and keep your heart going until more medical intervention can be arranged."

Imara's nervousness escalated, and a black streak moved past the cage to settle near her.

I am your first line of resuscitation, Mage. His black fur was spikey, and he was sitting a few feet away.

Eckoak frowned. "Your familiar is supposed to be in the antechamber."

Imara cleared her throat. "He is my first line of defense if I am injured. The medic can step in if my familiar steps back."

The dryad nodded reluctantly. "Acceptable. He just cannot assist you in your efforts."

"Don't worry. He is all in favour of my

falling flat on my face; he just doesn't want me dead."

"Fair enough. Now, once Medic Tellfirth is in his Faraday cage, I want you to strike your targets with lightning. You have the rest of class to make one large strike. The target will let me know when you have engaged in sufficient vigour in your strike."

Imara glanced at Kitty when two large, glowing orbs rose from the floor and settled about sixteen feet in the air, fifty feet away. It was going to be a very long morning.

Imara focused for half an hour, and only managed to create a spark that travelled two feet.

Eckoak was leaning against the podium and sipping her coffee, not offering any assistance and occasionally laughing at them.

Kitty was sitting and chanting. It was

her go to.

Imara looked at Kitty and her wealth of orbs then back to the target. Could it be that simple?

She looked at the orb and thought of it as a holding stone for a spectre. The power signature flared to life, and she nodded. "Right."

Another half hour had passed during her assessment, and Kitty was arcing lightning halfway to the target.

Imara raised her hands and charged them, holding them outward and calling the power from the target.

The energy rushed toward her, and she sent electricity back along the path. A crackle of lightning struck the orb, and it flared brilliant green.

She closed the link and sat down. Sweat was running down her spine, but Eckoak was grinning. One test done.

Kitty was still standing, her eyes focused and her hands forward. She had made a strike three-quarters of the way to the target, but she didn't trigger the target. She lacked power.

Kitty paused and flexed her fingers. The tips were bright red. She exhaled and looked at Imara. "I don't think I can manage this."

Imara smiled encouragingly and ran her hands through her hair before rubbing them on her thighs and back again. "I think you will get it. You just need to build up to it."

Kitty smiled and gave her a thumbs-up.

Imara waited on her mat while Kitty took off her shoes, walked off the rubber and rubbed her rings against her hair before buffing them against her thighs. She slowly built up her static charge, and when her hair was beginning to rise with the magical power, she stepped back onto the mat, conjured a small storm in her palms and then sent out a tremendous crack of lightning.

The target lit up and exploded.

Imara didn't cheer. She watched as Kitty stopped her storm and closed her hands, kneeling slowly. She drooped with fatigue, and when Eckoak moved toward her, Imara joined them.

Kitty lifted her head. "I did it."

Eckoak nodded and cupped her chin. "You did. Good call on the static. Pulling energy from nowhere to power lightning is usually very stupid. That is the reason for the medic. You two managed to get through it with some mild exhaustion. Well done, ladies, now go and get something to eat."

Imara helped Kitty to her feet, pausing to collect her shoes before heading for the door.

Mr. E ran ahead of them and was perched on her pack. She grabbed it with one hand and kept supporting Kitty as they got onto the lift.

"Come on, we are going to the Hall. I think you need a bit more than a sandwich."

Kitty nodded weakly. "Sounds great."

Mr. E sent a worried thought into Imara's mind. *I think I should run ahead and get Reegar to prepare something.*

Taking on more of Kitty's weight, Imara whispered, "I think that is an excellent idea."

He streaked off her shoulder the moment that they were above ground, and she watched his tail disappear down the path. She would have Kitty in a comfortable space in ten minutes if she could hold her up that long. She straightened her shoulders and hiked onward, with her friend stumbling gamely along.

Chapter Five

"**Y**our teacher should never have tried to get you to generate dry lightning. It was stupid." Reegar administered a draught to Kitty, forcing it down her though she fought the taste.

"It might have been, but we managed it."

"And she nearly drained herself of all vital energies in the process. I have seen this before, and it has had rather deadly outcomes."

Imara was manning the pot of soup that Reegar had pulled together. She watched the grumpy spectre taking care of her friend and fought a smile. "I knew I was doing the right thing when I came home."

"The draught will give her energy. Who is your instructor?"

Imara bit her lip. "Professor Eckoak. She's a very good elemental."

Reegar sneered. "Dryad. I know her. She was around the college as a student twenty years ago. She tried to plant a tree in my courtyard, and I sent her packing."

"Why was she here? The college is for mages, not extra-naturals."

"She evolved in her first year. Late bloomer. Her magic came on, and they didn't want to eject her, so they considered her an exchange student and waited to see if she would blend in."

"Did she?"

"No. But the issue of the tree was the only disagreement I had with her. I didn't hear much about her from the other building caretakers."

Kitty struggled to sit up straight.

"What was in that vial?"

Reegar glanced at her. "It was the vitamin shot that I work into all of Imara's food when she isn't looking. Nothing magical, just herbs and fruit extracts."

Imara suspected that he wasn't joking, but she asked, "Are you ready for some soup?"

"Yes, please. It smells great."

Mr. E came in, holding a metal charm in his mouth. He hopped up onto Kitty's lap and spat the charm out.

The light glow that came out of the charm was echoed in Kitty's eyes.

She blinked rapidly. "Wow, that feels much better."

She used her body to power the first strikes. It drained her. The harder she worked, the weaker she got.

Imara relayed the information to Kitty, and her friend nodded.

"Yeah, that is what it felt like."

She dished up some soup and put a

plate under it as well as some crackers on the plate. "Here you go."

Kitty set the plate in her lap, and she got to work on the soup.

Reegar smiled. "How is it?"

"Excellent. Thank you."

"My mother used to make it for me when I was in school. Of course, she made it over a coal fire, but I think the essence of the herbs come through."

The thought of Reegar having a mother had never really occurred to her. Imara cocked her head. "Did you always like to cook?"

"Always. It was relaxing to do something so ordinary, so human." He smiled. "Everybody has to eat."

"True. I hadn't thought of that. Cooking wasn't something that I bothered learning." She shrugged. "There was always something to study. Food just showed up, and I ate it."

Kitty smirked. "I had to come when I

was called, or I didn't eat."

Imara chuckled. "They had to feed me, or they didn't get paid."

Reegar glanced at her. "Was it awkward? You haven't mentioned your caretakers."

"It was rather cold. Even being here is warm and fuzzy by comparison, but then, I was always working toward a goal, and that didn't include them."

Kitty blinked. "You didn't live with your parents?"

"Nope. I am an off-contract birth. My father's family didn't want me, and my mother wasn't allowed to keep me. It all worked out." She said that in a rush when the stricken expression crossed over Kitty's face. "Really, it is all good. I have met my mother, and we get along very well. I have even met a few of my brothers. One is due here any minute, actually."

Kitty looked around. "Here?"

"Yup. Keep eating. He is dating Bara, and she has an early afternoon today. I am guessing he does as well because he is pulling up in the lot."

Kitty had just finished her restoring soup when Luken arrived.

Imara waved at him. "Hiya, Luken. This is Kitty. She is recovering from our morning class. Kitty, this is my brother, Luken Demiel."

Kitty looked from Imara to the young man standing beside her. "Well, he is definitely your brother."

Imara smiled. "Yeah, there is a resemblance."

Luken came up to her and nudged her on the arm. "This is my long-lost twin."

"I wasn't lost. I was merely misplaced." She laughed. "I found my way eventually."

"And I am glad you did. I wanted to see what my rugged good looks would be like on a lady. She isn't half bad."

Imara lifted her hand, held her thumb and forefinger apart and sent an arc of lightning from digit to digit. "I am not above zapping you, Luken."

He grinned. "Is Bara in?"

"No, but she should roll in in a few minutes. Her class is across campus, and it takes a while to haul all of her textile studies supplies home." She dismissed the energy and rubbed her palm on her thigh.

Luken nodded. "I will head out to help her. Nothing gets more bonus points than helping a damsel in distress. Kitty, it was a pleasure meeting you."

"Pleasure to meet you as well." Kitty nodded and waved as he headed back outside.

When he was gone, Kitty stared at Imara. "He is a third year."

"Yeah. He got early admission. How did you know?"

"My cousin was in a class with him,

and she had a huge crush. I have to admit, he's good looking."

Imara grinned. "He got the best side of the womb."

"Ah. Well, since I have my brain together for a moment, would you be interested in coming to my family's place next weekend? We have plenty of room, and my parents would love to meet you."

Imara blinked. "Um, why?"

We should go. I want to catch some shrews.

Imara looked at him. "Shrews?"

He yawned, showing his little white teeth. *They are all I can catch in this shape.*

Kitty smiled. "Yes, we have shrews. The yards are all hedged, so there are a bunch of small rodents around the property. We try and put up repulse spells, but they keep coming. So, Mr. E is interested?"

Imara sighed. "He is. I just am a little

unsure of how to deal with a family situation."

Kitty blinked. "Don't overthink it. We could practice mantras and poses in the old barn, and when my mom calls us for dinner, we go in and eat. When we are tired, we sleep. When the weekend is over, we come home. Nothing more than that."

"Why?"

"Because I really get the feeling that you need to do something not related to studying. We can go play with the lambs and calves if you like. Generally, you will just relax and unclench."

Reegar was fussing near the kitchen, and he turned back, "It might not be a bad idea. I think that you need a little socialization."

Imara stared at him. "I need to study."

He snorted. "You are already done with the paper courses for this term.

One weekend will do you good. You need to make more ties in the community than other students and your instructors."

"I have you and Bara."

He snorted again. "I am dead, and she is a career student. She isn't leaving here if she can help it."

Kitty was watching them and turning her head between them. "You are really a spectre?"

He bowed. "I most definitely am. Thanks to Imara's talents, I am solid and functioning within the confines of my territory."

"That's... amazing. What kind of spell does it?"

Imara looked at her. "Um, not a spell, just a benign energy output. I have an affinity for the dead."

Mr. E was sitting next to Kitty, and she was petting him absently. There was obviously something going on in her head.

Imara sat on the edge of the couch. "What is it?"

"I have a deceased member of the family that I would love to speak to. I know it is horrible to ask you to come for a fun visit and then ask a favour, but I haven't met someone who might be able to manage it before." Kitty looked down at Mr. E.

With a heavy sigh, she asked, "When do we leave?"

Kitty lifted her head and stared. "You will come?"

"Yes, I will. You will have to drive, but I will come. Is Mr. E going to be okay to come along?"

Mr. E hissed. *Where you go, I go. It's in my job description.*

Kitty nodded. "Of course. He will be welcome. Does he need any special food?"

Imara chuckled. "He does like pasta,

and you have seen him eat dessert."

Kitty laughed. "I will tell my family to lay in a little extra."

"Good. Send me the location details, so I can let my boyfriend know. He worries if I am left to my own devices for too long."

Kitty grabbed her phone, and Imara's chimed a moment later. When Imara checked the screen, a text gave her the address, the location, and the GPS coordinates.

"That was thorough."

Kitty smiled. "Just in case you want to forward it to anyone. Better to discard some information than to not have it in the first place."

Kitty took one of her spheres off her necklace, and she dangled it in front of Mr. E.

"That isn't a good idea." Just as she finished the warning, Mr. E had batted the small orb out of her fingers and was chasing it around the carpet in front of the couch.

The kitten had once again won over the familiar, and it was a great thing to watch for an hour or so.

When Kitty was getting ready to leave, Imara asked, "So, what do I need to bring?"

"Yourself and clothing that you don't mind getting dirty. Farms are farms, and the best places to hang out and be quiet involve a little hike through woods and streams."

Imara nodded, and when Kitty was gone, she turned to Reegar. "I don't hike."

He laughed, dissipated, and she was left trying to find her familiar under the couch. A mage's work was never done.

Chapter Six

Imara held Mr. E on her lap as Kitty pulled her truck down a drive and the white fences that contained green meadows and distant large animals were on either side of the truck.

The kitten hopped up on his hind legs and looked out the truck window with his tail lashing.

Can I chase them?

Imara chuckled. "No. Stick to rodents and birds. If this weekend goes well, we might want to ask to come back."

His tail lashed. *Best behaviour then. Got it.*

Kitty grinned. "He dreams of chasing sheep?"

"I think he dreams of chasing elephants. His dreams are big."

Kitty nodded, and they spent the next few minutes drawing closer to the main farm.

"This place is huge." Imara was amazed.

"It needs to be. Cows are big, and sheep love to run."

The main house loomed up in front of them, and the cheerful white was dotted with a series of gleaming orbs.

"Oh, right. Family talent."

"Yeah, we can always tell where one of us is."

"Do you have a large family?"

"Our branch? No. but there are Deegles around the country." Kitty's rings flashed as she curved the truck in a slow arc and they stopped twenty feet from the main house. "We're here. Welcome to my home."

They exited her truck, and Mr. E was

quivering with the urge to explore.

Imara whispered, "Be careful and keep our link open. Call me if you need help."

It was all he needed to know. The kitten streaked across the property and headed for the meadow that Kitty had identified as belonging to the sheep.

Imara sighed. "I hope he is on good behaviour."

Kitty chuckled and got their bags, holding Imara's out to her. "He will be fine. Cats are on the farm all the time. They live in the barn."

"He isn't actually a cat, though, and he hasn't had any large prey to chase for a while."

Kitty paused. "How big?"

Imara sighed. "I shouldn't have said anything."

"Is he dangerous?"

"Only if I am threatened, otherwise, he is a pussycat."

"Good. He will be fine here then. There isn't anything to harm him or you at the farm. Well, unless you try and milk the bull. Then, you get what you deserve." Kitty laughed.

Imara winced. "I will try not to milk anything while I am here. I think it is just a safer practice."

Kitty grinned and led the way to the big house. A black flash streaked across the green in the distance, and Imara's mind was filled with giggles. At least he was already having a good time.

The door to the main house opened, and a man approached them, wiping his hands on a dishtowel and sporting a smear of flour on his cheek. "You made excellent time."

Kitty hugged him. "Nice to see you, too, Dad. This is Imara Mirrin. Imara, this is my dad, Andrew Deegle."

Imara stepped forward and extended her hand. The handshake was warm and firm, Andrew's callouses were heavy enough to hurt, but he watched his grip.

She smiled. "I am pleased to meet you, Mr. Deegle."

"Andy, please. I am delighted to meet you as well. Kitigan doesn't make many friends."

Kitty wiggled her fingers with their multitude of rings. "I'm too sparkly."

Imara laughed. "I think it is your propensity to tell folks you can see the future. It either repulses or intrigues."

Andy asked, "What did it do for you?"

"It made me relax. I hadn't met anyone else with a properly weird talent until she showed up." She chuckled. "Kitty keeps it interesting without having to discuss her talent all the time, once she knew I wasn't going to pester her for a reading."

Andy looked at her. "You have really never wanted to see your future?"

Imara shrugged. "Nope. My past is

past, and my future will decide itself. No sense rushing the identification of trauma or joy."

"That is a very mature attitude."

She wrinkled her nose. "Not really. I just hate most surprises and knowing that they were coming would make the anticipation worse."

"No worries around here. The worst thing to anticipate is a stray sheep." He inclined his head. "Consider yourself at home."

Kitty shifted from foot to foot. "Can I show her to the guestroom?"

Andy shook his head. "Given that she has a familiar, I have pulled out our newest acquisition."

There was an ear-shattering squeal from Kitty, she grabbed Imara's hand and hauled her around the far side of the house where a micro house was perched with connections to water and power.

"It was on order when I started the

term. It is even cuter than I imagined."

"It's a tiny house."

"That it is. Come on. I have been dying to see inside." Kitty opened the door, and Imara followed her into the building.

The space was well organized. A small desk against the wall had a padded stool tucked under it, the bed was in a loft, and the kitchen had regular-sized appliances.

"This place is nice. Is that a quilt?" Imara climbed the ladder to check the bed. She tucked her bag next to the mattress and ran a hand over the patchwork fabric. "It's lovely."

"My mother made it. She makes and sells stuff on the internet, and this is one of her crafts." Kitty stood on the ladder and looked over the object that Imara was stroking.

"It's amazing. I have seen this kinda thing online, but never up close." The geometric patterns wove one piece into the other, and the stitching that held them together added texture and strength. A symphony in blue and purple, and she got to sleep under it that night.

Imara looked to Kitty, "Will they mind Mr. E up here?"

"Of course not. That is one reason they offered you privacy. Mages with familiars are more sensitive to strange environments. This one is all yours while you are here, but you can still eat with us in the main house."

Imara smiled. "Can I see the rest of the property?"

"Sure. Did you want to ride horses? It will make it easier."

Excitement stirred. "I haven't ridden a horse before."

"This is an excellent time to start. The horses won't tell a soul if you are a little stiff."

Imara approached the ladder, and when Kitty moved back, she climbed down to the main floor. "Lead the way. My humiliation awaits."

"I won't tell if you don't tell my parents that I tried to make lightning using my own energy. In hindsight, it was a very stupid move."

"You are not wrong."

Imara grinned as Kitty huffed and led the way out of the tiny structure and across the yard toward the large barn.

"So, you ride horses a lot?"

"Sure. There is no better way to get around this kind of terrain. They can fuel themselves if they need it."

Imara couldn't argue. The scent of hay and animals came to her on the wind as they reached the barn.

"I will go in and see who needs exercise. You can wait out here if you like."

"No, I would like to see how this is done. I imagine it is different in reality than it is on television."

Kitty shrugged and hauled the door open. "Not really. Sure, there are a few more bits to attach to the horses, but the key is to make everything comfortable and secure for horse and rider."

They walked into the dim interior, and Kitty headed for a shed in the rear of the building. Imara followed, passing stalls where curious heads poked over their doors, giving her a long look. Imara inclined her head formally and kept following the other human in the building.

"So, how do you tell who needs exercise?"

Kitty grinned. "We don't ask them if that is what you are getting at. We check the schedule. Every time we take a horse out, we make a note of the date and duration, as well as anything awkward on the ride. It helps the vets as well. We can track an illness in the animals if we have to, back to the day it happened. Sometimes, it is even naturally occurring plants that cause an issue."

"Oh."

Kitty blushed. "Sorry. I am just excited to have a visitor with me. You wouldn't believe some of the views we are going to ride through."

"Gotcha. I get the same way talking about the dead. It is exciting but only from a certain angle." Imara grinned. "Ignore me. I am eager to learn how to do this."

"In that case, let me pick a good mount for you, and then, you can carry the tack to the stall."

"Yes, ma'am. I am throwing myself on your mercy."

"Good plan. I have your comfort for the rest of the day at my discretion." She checked a clipboard on the wall and looked down the line of stalls. "I think that Bright Bell is a good choice for you.

He is friendly and good-natured, as well as an excellent trail horse. He can find his way home on his own. All you need to do is hang on."

"Great. That's encouraging."

"It should be. Some of these ladies or gentlemen would dump you in a ravine and run off giggling or the horsy equivalent."

That was a warning as much as encouragement. Kitty picked her own mount and then, they were into the tack room to get the leather straps and saddles that would hold them in place.

Imara watched the process in amazement as Kitty tucked, buckled, strapped, and tugged at the leather until their horses were standing and ready for them.

The instructions of how to lead Bright Bell out and into the yard were a blur as Imara focused on the huge creature that she was holding by a flimsy strap. It seemed friendly enough and nudged her lightly.

"He likes you. That's a good thing."

"Oh. Good."

"Are you ready to get on?"

Imara inhaled and exhaled slowly. "Yup."

"Good. Gather the reins in your left hand, keep them firm but loose, so they don't pull his head. Left foot into the stirrup, hand on the pommel, and haul yourself up while bringing your right leg over. He is a patient horse, so take your time. He can hold you."

Imara looked at the satiny grey hide and the calm brown eyes. She nodded, arranged the reins, and used all of her yoga practice to get her foot high enough to reach the stirrup. The grip on the saddle and heaving herself upward was done in a controlled rush. A few seconds later, she was blinking in surprise at her new point of view. She stroked Bright

Bell's neck and whispered, "Thanks."

He shifted slightly, and she let her hips move with him. She was going to be sore tomorrow, but this was another experience to add to her collection.

Kitty got up onto her mount gracefully, and she turned the chestnut horse and walked back to Imara. "Slip your right foot into the stirrup, if he increases his pace, use the stirrups to get your butt off the saddle or be jolted into bits, but otherwise, let me guide and he will follow. You just have to look at the scenery."

Imara remained calm while her ride started moving. She hoped that Mr. E was having fun in the fields. She was on her own little journey of exhilaration; she just didn't have another life waiting if something went wrong.

Chapter Seven

The view was amazing. No matter which way she turned, Imara saw beauty and life.

Kitty rode ahead of her, and her ease in the saddle was apparent. Aside from envy, Imara had a few things she needed to ask, so she steeled herself and made her move. It took a bit of goading, but Imara got Bright Bell to draw even with Kitty's mount.

"So, Kitty, who did you need me to work with?"

Kitty looked confused. "What?"

"The spectre."

"Oh. It's a long story, but the end of it is my grandfather."

"I need a bit more information, please."

Kitty sighed. "Twenty years ago, my grandfather passed, and my grandmother didn't take it well. She was an orb seer, just like my father and me, so she began to stare into the future. She took the master orb that my dad had made and poured her energy into it. In that orb, she saw my grandfather holding her hand once again. Ever since, she spends her days looking five minutes into the future, looking for him."

"Oh damn."

"Right, so you see the problem."

"Did you put your grandfather to rest as a mage?"

"We did. I mean, I was a child, but my mother says that his gravesite is properly cared for."

Imara sighed. "I will have to talk to your parents about his effects. I can use one of the retaining stones and his link to your grandmother to bring him out, but only if the connection is strong on all counts."

Kitty looked hopeful. "You actually think you can do it?"

"If the proper rituals were engaged in when he passed, yes. It is easy." Imara had a thought. "You were right about the Mage Guides. They are eager to have me volunteer by taking a tour through a cemetery in order to talk to some spectres."

Kitty smirked. "Thought so. It is a neglected area of mage-craft just because we can't get anyone to show us around. It is always depicted as creepy, just because it is unknown."

Bright Bell stiffened under her, and Imara looked around to see what had gotten his attention.

"Damn. Dad said they had moved in, but I was hoping that they weren't this far to the edge of their territory yet." Kitty's mood shifted suddenly as she stared at the brush in the valley below.

"Is something here?"

"A new werewolf pack split and left their elders and are now running around on the fifty acres to the west of our property line." She grimaced. "It is nowhere near enough space for them, but it is what was available."

Imara stared at the edge of the treeline, and within it, she could see the flicker of shadows and flash of silver fur. "Don't those trees abut your property line?"

"The first row on our side is the windbreak."

The horses shifted restlessly. Kitty got her mount under control, but Imara had to focus as Bright Bell got nervous. "Easy, dude."

"We had better turn back."

Kitty had no sooner mentioned it than a howl broke free of the woods and a rush of dark fur came toward them.

Bright Bell reared and tossed his head before turning and bolting toward the barn. Imara's grip on the saddle kept her in place during the jarring sprint, but a glance back showed that the wolves were waiting on the ridge, defending what they considered to be their territory. This required investigation as soon as she got her butt of the leather that was being pounded into it.

Kitty and her mount beat them to the barn, and she held Bright Bell while Imara slithered off with the grace of a bag of pudding.

"You go and grab a hot shower. I will take care of the horses."

She nodded and headed for the tiny house with the intent of contacting Argus. If anyone knew what was going on and what could be done about werewolves encroaching on territories, it would be another shifter.

When she dragged herself out of the shower, wrapped in a towel, the flashing light on her phone told her that Argus was up.

She called him and smiled at the rumble of his voice.

"What have you gotten yourself into, Imara?"

"Nothing. Just a little light territorial encroachment by a pack on a local farmer. I want to know what I am able to do to defend the space."

"Can't the farmer do it? He has the right."

"I don't think so. He is mainly a seer, and his daughter is still in school with me."

She could almost sense his brain heating up while he worked out what he would say next.

"Technically, they are responsible for their defense, but if they offer you a legal foothold for yourself or your power, you can act on their behalf.”

“Wow. It is like you are a seer yourself. I have that very setup, or will by the end of the evening. So, I am allowed to defend this place?”

“By any means necessary. Call me if things escalate beyond posturing. I may not be able to come, but I can get a local XIA detachment to send someone out.”

“I will.”

“And Imara? Take care of yourself. This could get dangerous very quickly.”

“I will. Thanks for the consultation, Argus. I owe you dinner when I get home.”

“You don’t cook.”

“But you are a very brave soul. I am sure that I can figure something out.” She grinned, her soul bubbling a little as it always did when she talked to him.

“Make sure that Mr. E is nearby if you want to do anything really stupid. He knows his job.”

"Yes, Agent Argus."

"I mean it. I worry about you." His tone was low.

"I know. I don't mean to get into trouble, but it seems to seek me out."

"Well, at least you are lucky."

She smirked. "Of course, I am. I met you, didn't I?"

His laugh was wry. "Yeah, you did, and I am willing to pay the price for the association. Be on guard but be cautious. I am going to look into the pack that has moved in and see if I can get you any more information."

"I await your update. Have a good shift. Don't let the boys eat too many tacos. You know that trolls have delicate digestion."

"Don't remind me. Have a fun evening. I should have details in a few hours."

Imara smiled and disconnected the call. They didn't say goodbye, just like they didn't need to say hello. Their communication was just one long conversation interrupted by time. Nothing could, or would, separate them. Part of her had realized it the moment that they met.

She got dressed in fresh clothing and went in search of Kitty. Mr. E sauntered up to her, and she lifted him to put him on her shoulder.

"Dude, you smell like sheep."

I was making friends. They are very friendly sheep.

She rolled her eyes and found Kitty in the barn, brushing Bright Bell and soothing him. The horse was still quivering with upset.

Let me speak to him.

Imara approached and cleared her throat. "Mr. E is going to chat with Bright Bell."

The kitten walked from her shoulder to the top of the stall door.

Kitty paused in her ministrations when the horse visibly calmed. "What is he saying?"

"I have no idea. He is speaking via his kitten side, so I am not privy to it. It isn't anything bad though. Bright Bell looks calmer already."

The horse in question moved forward and pressed his long nose to Imara's shoulder. He nipped gently at her sleeve, and she stroked his head.

"Well, whatever he said worked. All of the horses are relaxed and at ease." Andy's voice was low and calm. "Ladies, time to wash up for dinner."

Kitty nodded, and Imara finished petting Bright Bell as her friend exited the stall.

Mr. E hopped back onto her shoulder, and they left the barn where the animals were diving into their dinners and went to find their own.

The family dinner table was something that Imara had heard of but never experienced firsthand. Meals at the hall were generally had around the table in the library or in the common room.

Dishes were set around the table, and everyone had a place. Kitty's mother showed her the seat that was set aside for guests. "Here you go, just call out if anything is out of your reach."

"I will. Thank you. It smells wonderful."

"Thank you. It is delightful to have a friend of Kitigan's here at the farm."

"It has been fun so far. Thank you for having me." She went through the rituals that Bara had drummed into her.

"Oh, I am May, by the way."

"Pleased to meet you, May. Your daughter has been an excellent study partner."

Kitty came in, shaking her hands. "Don't listen to that. Imara is an amazing and natural mage. Anyone near her gets better by simple proximity."

"Can you get your grandmother?"

"She is washing up. Is she any better?" Kitty looked worried.

"She is as she has been."

Imara cleared her throat. "I have some questions to ask about her husband, if I may."

May looked at her for a moment. "After dinner is soon enough when my mother-in-law has resumed her watch on the future."

Imara nodded, and when the elder Deegle appeared, she introduced herself to the vague and unfocused woman.

Dinner conversation was polite and centred around the class that Kitty and Imara were taking. Weather was a large concern on the farm.

When the grandmother rose and headed back to her attic room, Imara sighed, "All right. I hate to ask, but what measures were taken when Mr. Deegle passed away? Was his spectre stone generated? Are there any artifacts to anchor him? Where is he buried?"

May looked confused, but Andy cleared his throat. "We have the spectre stone, but we didn't anchor it."

Imara made a face. "Right. Okay."

"We have enough personal effects to fill a room. This entire property was his selection. They moved here, and May and I moved in with them when we married. The land was perfect for both our family needs."

"Would you mind having his spectre around?" It was an important question, and she watched them carefully.

Andy nodded his head slowly. "I would like to be able to speak with him again."

May asked the pertinent question, "Would the spectre outlast Anna? I couldn't bear it if she lost him again."

Imara smiled. "I can anchor him to the land and give you directions for his slow dissolve after she passes. If you choose to keep him, he can be a permanent guardian."

Kitty blinked. "You talk about him like he's a dog."

Imara rubbed her jaw. "His soul is gone; this is a copy of his emotion and intellect. He knows he's dead, but I can give him enough energy to keep him solid when he wants to be. His spirit can roam this land and watch over it if you like. It would just involve a lot of rock and some planted trees."

Andy stared at her. "It is that easy?"

"Well, if you are a Death Keeper, yes. The primary issue is the generating site. Where do you want to keep him and talk to him directly?"

Andy got up from the table, and he returned in a moment with a map. He moved dishes aside and opened it up.

"Here. We always meant to install the stone here, but it is so expensive to get a private installation."

"Right. I am going to need a hammer, chisel, the spectre stone, and a bunch of pebbles or river rocks. The trees can be planted later."

May asked, "Do you need it by midnight?"

"Well, I would like to head to bed before eleven, so the sooner, the better. Time isn't a factor, and we could do it tomorrow morning if you wanted. I just thought that having him here tonight would be a good start."

The Deegles shot out in different directions, and Imara prepared another plate for Mr. E.

Why are you doing this? It will take a lot of energy.

"They are in pain. An entire family is in pain, and I can fix it. That doesn't cost me anything but slight dizziness and a few hours of focus. I will be fine in the morning, and I can send them powered items as they need it."

They are mages, and hundreds of families can't afford what you are about to do, are you going to do it for all of them?

"The ones that I meet face to face, sure. Just imagine, we can come back here for maintenance and you can chase more sheep."

Point taken. Focus. You are going to connect some very rusty dots. This I have got to see.

With that encouragement, she started the inner chant that would focus the energy she needed to wake the spectre stone and bind it to the rock. She was going to need another meal when it was over or maybe just some pie.

Chapter Eight

$\mathcal{T}$he box was carved with designs, and she could feel the magic humming inside it. It was a holding box, and the glyphs were designed to keep the consciousness as fresh as the day that the deceased passed on. It was a bit unpleasant to think of it in such terms, but the spectre she was going to be releasing was not the original man. It was a copy.

The Deegles were waiting for her. She could hear the tapping in the rock to prime the hole. She would do most of the work, but a niche to start with was always appreciated.

Imara looked down at her robes. Packing them had been a whim based on what Kitty had mentioned. Now, Imara realized that they were at least two inches too short. She had grown since she started as apprentice.

Are you ready for this?

"Yeah. I have done this before."

I thought you had to be a master before you activated a spectre.

"Only if the family is watching. This isn't a first for me."

Well, well. The more I live in the modern age, the more I learn. Are you ready?

"Stop asking that. Yes. I am ready. Here we go."

She opened the door with the box held carefully in her left hand. Leaving the small house was symbolic. It was a neutral site that had nothing to do with the family. There were no ties for the spectre to attach to, so it was the safest place to start from, just in case she activated him early. It wasn't going to happen, but protocol meant that someone had been stupid at some point.

She crossed the yard with Mr. E at her side, heading up slope from the house and against the trees, geographically in the centre of the property.

The family was waiting, even the grandmother was standing with her burned-out orbs on her fingers, around her neck, and held in her hands.

Andy was standing with the hammer and chisel in his hands.

Imara smiled, "Please set the tools down."

He nodded nervously and set the tools at the base of the stone that held the chisel marks.

"Does anyone here not wish to see the spectre of the deceased?"

The family looked at each other, and they shook their heads. Andy cleared his throat. "We are in agreement. We want as much of him as we can have."

"Very well. I will let you know when you can speak to him. Please, allow me to work without interruption."

They nodded again and stepped back. The grandmother was watching her with fascination, so Imara smiled to her before she picked up the implements and set to work.

The first strike took her an inch into the hard rock. The second made the cavity she needed. With care and reverence, she opened the box and removed the stone that carried the residue of the man who was beloved by those around her.

Imara took the glowing gem and rammed it into the cavity in the stone. The rock melted as she focused on joining the stone and the gem together.

When her hand felt the burn, she pulled her palm away. Now, it was time to do her part as a Death Keeper.

She whispered to him, drawing him out, calling him to the objects he had left behind. She appealed to his love and the wedding ring that was sitting on velvet within the box.

It took an hour to pull the consciousness from the stone, but when she felt him release into the bedrock around her, she stood back and smiled.

"Anderson Morden Deegle, you are requested to join us."

The spectre emerged from the stone and took form. Anna gasped and sobbed, May had tears in her eyes, and so did her husband. Kitty was simply in shock.

"Death Keeper, how did you come to be here?" Anderson Deegle turned his head. He was still transparent, but his voice came through.

"I am a student who shares a weather magic class with your granddaughter, Kitigan. She is an adult now, and as I was here for a weekend off, I am repaying my hosts with your rejuvenation."

He nodded. "What about when you leave? How quickly will I fade?"

"You won't. I will plant power nodes around the property tomorrow, and you will be able to walk the farm again, even hold Anna's hand again if you wish."

"Anna." The longing in the voice was obvious.

"Yes, she is waiting for you. She has seen this moment and has spent twenty years waiting for it."

He looked around and spotted his wife. "Anna."

Tears filled her eyes, and she dropped the glass in the grass. "Anderson. Is it really you?"

Imara poured her death magic into him, turning the translucent body into something far more solid.

"Anna." The spectre reached for her and then paused.

Anna didn't hesitate, she held his hands, and when she felt the solid warmth of him, she sobbed and threw herself against him.

Imara looked to Kitty. "Did you get those rocks I asked for?"

Kitty nodded, and her gaze darted around until she found what she was looking for. She moved past Imara and grabbed a large pail from next to the stone. "Here they are."

"Thanks. I am going to take these back to the tiny house. In the morning, if you are up to it, we can take another ride and anchor Anderson to the property. He can then come and go as he pleases or wherever you please. He will be able to reach the edges of your property."

Andy was hugging the spectre of his father, and the joyful and tearful reunion was heartwarming.

"Yeah, you introduce yourself to your grandfather. I have to have a nap with rocks next to me. Ah, the life of a Death Keeper is so glamorous."

Grinning but tired, Imara headed back to her tiny sanctuary.

Mr. E trotted along on his little legs, keeping up with her tired steps.

I thought that enhancing spectres didn't exhaust you.

"It doesn't, but fusing and raising one does. Tomorrow will be easy in comparison. All I need tonight is a good night's sleep."

It was as if she was casting a curse.

The howl brought her out of bed in a heartbeat. Imara rolled to the floor and sat blinking as she fought to figure out where she was.

The huffing and growling around the tiny house warned her that the wolves were in her territory.

Those little bastards. Do you want me to hurt them?

Imara spoke silently, "No, I want to take care of this myself. They are young, not homicidal."

The door to the roof opened from the upper loft, and she slid out, removing her nightgown as she did. She gathered her focus and launched herself from the roof, shifting form as she fell.

The first wolf that had her full vulture weight went to the ground with a grunt. She pecked and pulled, tearing a strip off his neck. Another launch and she got the second wolf.

The third moved so that she was on the ground and couldn't launch. Imara wasn't having any of that, so she shifted and jumped at the bugger, pinning him to the ground as her form slowly became fully human.

"Naughty fellas. This isn't your property, and it sure as fuck isn't your territory. If you come back here, I will be much less polite."

She levered herself off the wolf, and he and her two victims ran back to their territory.

Imara stretched, and when she heard a small cough, she turned to see the family staring at her. Kitty was bright pink and pale at the same time.

Imara grinned. "I will get back to bed."

Andy raised his brows, "I didn't know you were a shapeshifter."

"Last term. Top of my class. It isn't a glamorous shape, but I am definitely comfortable as a vulture. The nudity is literally par for the course."

He nodded and herded the ladies back into the house. May turned back. "Thank you. I dread to think of what they would have done to us."

"Just peed on you. That is their big move. My tearing a strip off them will follow them into their human form. It is one of the annoying little bits of etiquette that you have to learn when you change shape."

Kitty looked as if she wanted to ask a question, but she was tucked inside the house.

Imara opened the door of the tiny house and returned to bed. Mr. E had pulled her nightgown off the roof, and he was using it as a cat bed.

She was tired enough that she didn't really care.

Over breakfast the questions started.

"How do you learn to change shape?"

Imara cocked her head at Kitty. "You study for it. Not everyone makes it, and many are stuck in forms that would haunt your nightmares."

Kitty shuddered.

Imara slathered some butter on her bread and tore the bread apart to dunk in her egg yolk.

May cleared her throat. "How is it that you have such a variety of skills at so young an age?"

Imara smiled. "That one is easy. I had nothing to do but focus on my future, so when I was given access to magic, I dove into it with my entire being. For my ultimate goal, I need to get through college with a degree as fast as I can. I have set my sights on courses that offer multiple credits because of their difficulty and that included the shapeshifting course."

Kitty blinked, "Is that how you met your boyfriend?"

"No. We were in an ethics course. He was taking it for work, and for me, it is a requirement to getting my magical consulting license."

May asked, "Consulting?"

"Yeah, I want to be a spectral consultant. Since Death Keepers are so few and far between and I am already a registered member of their guild, it is just a matter of getting the Mage Guild to accept me as a commercial member and I am on my way."

"You would do things like you did last night?"

"Like wrestle wolves naked? Not usually, but I could and would pull a few more coherent thoughts out of the spectres, no matter how old."

The family nodded and paused when Anna came in with Anderson at her side. They both were glowing with happiness, and it wasn't in Imara's nature to ask why.

Kitty, however, hissed, "Can they do *that?*"

Imara grinned. "It takes a lot of effort on his part, but yeah, they can."

Andy chuckled. "It was how he died. They had a great sex life right until the last."

Anna smiled, focused, and in the moment. "And it is back."

Imara blushed at the hot look that the grandmother was giving the spectre, twenty years her junior.

The worst thing was the reciprocation. He was seeing her as she was, and he obviously thought she was hot.

The eternal bond of love had never taken physical form for her before. She wondered if she and Argus would still be looking at each other with that intensity when they were old enough to retire? She really hoped so.

Chapter Nine

"So, what are we going to do about the wolves?" Kitty asked it as if she was solely responsible for carrying out a hit. They were out on the ridge where the wolves had made their run the day before.

"We are going to keep planting these stones. Once they are in place, Anderson can keep them out."

"Why is my mom calling the local arborists?"

Imara knelt at the first site she had identified as a good point of support. "Because on their own, these stones act as a battery for your grandfather. With the trees living and carrying the signal, it is like Wi-Fi. He can appear and act within several hundred feet of one of those trees."

"So, in theory, he is the ultimate watchman."

"Yes. Spectres love being useful. The majority of degradation happens when they have nothing to do. They just let their energies float back into the aether or whatever you want to call it."

Bright Bell was nearby and waiting patiently with his reins on the ground. Imara smiled at the picture he made with Mr. E perching on the saddle. After the first ride, he wasn't letting her out on her own again. She didn't mind. He obviously had more experience with horses than she did.

Humming to herself, Imara dug a hole a foot deep and as narrow as she could make it. When it was ready, she dropped in one of the rocks, covered it up, and sighted for the next target.

"Okay. Off we go."

"Is that it? You don't have to chant or cast a spell?"

"No, proximity to me has charged them, and it will keep him running as long as you need him, or until the energy fades after I die."

"Oh. Wow."

Imara got back on her horse, and they started the slow amble to the next site. "Does the future you see stop being possible because you aren't paying attention or you haven't cast a spell?"

"Um, no."

"Same difference. It is just what happens around me. It was freaky at first, but I am simply used to it now."

Kitty grinned, and she checked the map. "I have the next one."

"Be my guest." Imara watched as Kitty urged her horse to a faster pace to get to the next site.

It went fairly briskly after that. They

hopscotched around the property until it buzzed with spectral energy. There were less than a dozen sites to go when Anderson appeared in front of them.

"Kitigan, you and Imara are needed at the house. The XIA are here."

Imara looked to Kitty and shrugged. "I think we are on our way. We should be there in five minutes."

He nodded and winked at his granddaughter. "See you shortly."

Kitty looked at Imara wide-eyed. "What do you think they want?"

"I am guessing they are reporting a shifter-on-shifter attack from last night. Or they are complaining about the spectre on your property. In the latter case, I filed the registration this morning after I brushed my teeth and before breakfast, and if it is the former... I am not a shapeshifter by nature." To be sure, she sent a text to Argus asking for his advice. It was after noon, and he was an early riser for his evening shifts, so there was a chance he would get back to her.

You will be fine. You have done nothing wrong.

"I know, but I still like to have my facts straight as for what I am and am not allowed to do."

It is a habit that has served you well. I have your back if needed.

Kitty was tense and curious. Imara had to guess she didn't run into the XIA that frequently.

They rode in silence, and the collection of vehicles in the yard was visible when they were still a few minutes out.

"Oh, look. A parade."

"How can you make jokes? You could be in trouble."

"Could be, but I haven't done anything that isn't allowed by their own regulations. I checked."

Their horses ambled right into the collection of irate wolves and the black-garbed XIA representatives.

The shifter officer took point. "Which of you is the shifter?"

Imara leaned on the pommel of the saddle and raised her brows. "I am not a shifter, but I am a mage who passed the course with one form."

"I am putting you under arrest for assault of a minor."

She looked over at the smug teens, two of whom were wearing bandages on their necks. "I really don't think so."

The man snarled. "Get off that horse."

"Sure, but I am still not under arrest. By shifter community standards, a non-shifter is within their rights to defend themselves with non-lethal force. They came into my territory and tried to mark it as their own, so I marked them. It isn't anything that won't heal and is definitely something that my shape does naturally."

The teens looked a little nervous.

The agent backed off slightly. "What do you mean?"

"I mean that I was offered the tiny house over there as my home while I was visiting, and as such, when howling and milling wolves circled it at night, putting on my beast and letting them know what I thought of them was within my rights."

The agent turned to Andy. "Did you give her the house?"

"For the extent of her stay and anytime she wishes to use it. That is her home and her property whenever she is here."

The agent got a little frustrated. His teammate came forward and pushed him back with a gentle shove. "Apologies, miss, but we have to look into this."

She inclined her head to the fey. "I am guessing that their complaint was that I either used magic or attacked them unprovoked?"

"And that you attacked them while they were in human form."

She snorted. "I can prove that one right now." She lifted the edge of her t-shirt where a criss-cross hatch mark of wolf claw residue was raised in red on her skin. "Last time I checked, toes didn't grow that close together on a human form."

All of the males in the area with the exception of Andy and Anderson were staring at her pale skin marked with red welts.

"And, miss, if I may, what is your beast?"

She grinned. "Gryphon vulture."

The wolf officer paled and whirled on what appeared to be his relatives. He began speaking rapidly, growling and cursing them out for being cowardly little pups who didn't deserve to be sneaking around on their own territory.

The parents of the youngsters were

shocked. One mother spluttered, "But what about the sexual assault?"

Imara paused, stunned. "The what?"

The woman stiffened her spine and glared at her. "The sexual assault. Henry said you were all over him and he had to fight you off."

Imara grunted. "Right. Of course. Did he also mention that in shifted form I am a *fucking bird?* He was coming in for attack, so I had to shift to defend myself. If you would like to examine the residue outside the tiny house, the claw and footprints tell the tale. I mean, unless you have a way to change shape with your clothing on, and you can fight off an attacker without touching them. It was his claws that made the marks on my abdomen. I don't think I left any on him."

The mother blinked. "Can I see the site?"

Imara looked at the elf and cocked

her head. "Care to come with?"

"I believe it would be wise. Jerry doesn't seem quite himself today."

Imara nodded and walked toward the tiny house with her micro-entourage and Mr. E at her side.

"You seem very well possessed for a woman your age."

"Um, thanks, I guess. I have had a lot of practice." Her phone pinged.

What are the names of the agents?

"Can I ask the names of your team?"

"I am Noro, there is also Agent Wells and Agent Atrico."

"Cool, just a moment." She keyed in the names and sent them.

She was walking them through the events from the roof to the ground when Argus pinged back. *Stay away from Noro. He's a perv.*

Funny, he doesn't look pervy.

He has a girl in every town, sometimes two.

Jealous?

Hell no. I can wait.

"Who are you texting? You have an amazing expression on your face." Agent Noro was right beside her, his silky hair sliding over his shoulder and the scent of wild flowers riding along with it.

"My boyfriend. He's concerned and a bit frustrated that he can't smooth this over."

"Ah, a pity." Noro gave her a long, slow look via his rich purple eyes.

"Not really. I usually do pretty well on my own." She smiled. "Now, what is your verdict on the situation?"

"Well, I can taste the blood and magic of the shifters here, as well as the marks of your claws. What I can also sense is a spectre in the area, and there isn't a registration on file."

She blinked. "There isn't? Huh. Check again."

He raised one pale brow and checked

his database. The new entry was marked in hot purple. Imara could see it over his shoulder.

"Master Mirrin. My apologies for not giving you your title."

She wrinkled her nose. "He was my qualifier. It is difficult to find a stored situation that hasn't been installed."

"I don't understand."

"I was an apprentice authorized to make spectres last night, and with my fifth installation behind me, I am now a Master."

"Ah. Congratulations. Would you like to celebrate?"

She grinned. "No."

He blinked and leaned back. "No?"

"Correct. I have chosen my mate, and you are not him. I choose not to dabble."

"That is... unusual."

She shrugged. "That is my personal choice. Respect it."

Noro looked more intrigued than perturbed. "I certainly do, but should our paths cross again, I will definitely be checking to make sure that you have not engaged in your prerogative of changing your mind."

The mother was looking at the traces of the scuffle, and she was getting angry. With a brisk nod to Imara, she headed back to the group.

Imara watched her stance and winced. "From previous observation, that pose means that someone is going to get it."

The hand that slapped the young, un-injured man across the face was wielded with righteous indignation. The man stumbled and went down on one knee while his mother grabbed him by the back of his neck and shook him with a lot more power than a human mother would have mustered.

The adult males let her rave on about how her son had not only risked his own life but the lives of mages and seers who had been nothing but polite neighbours.

She hissed at him, and the young male grovelled, begging for forgiveness from Andy.

"I am sorry that I brought my pack to your door. Please forgive me." He had his head bowed, but the rest of him was standing tall.

"You did not assault me or insult me. You owe your words to my guest." Andy extended his hand toward Imara.

The resentment in the young man's gaze should have scalded, but Imara looked at him with what she hoped was an impassive expression.

He turned his head and didn't step toward her, but she let out a sharp yip that made the assembled werewolves jump. He stared at her and walked to her, kneeling in front of her.

"I am sorry for infringing on your territory. It was wrong, it was stupid, and I am deeply sorry for any injury I caused or that my pack caused you."

"Sorry that you saw me naked?"

He looked up and flashed a quick grin. "No, but if there is anything I can do to make up for the injuries, I would be happy to oblige."

She cocked her head. "Are you serious?"

He nodded. "I am. We overstepped our territory, and it will not happen again."

Imara looked to May. "Are the trees on the way?"

May caught on quickly. "They will be here within the hour."

Imara then turned to Noro, "The charges of assault and trespassing will be dropped if they work it off. We have trees to plant, and the more hands to the task the better."

The father cleared his throat. "We were not charging for the assault."

Agent Noro nodded. "She has it right. There is nothing to charge her with. She was perfectly within her rights to act as she did and well within her rights to kill the pack."

The adults paled. Henry's mother stepped forward, "Thank you, miss, for not doing more than you did. They are young, they are stupid, and they are learning. You will have them until your task is complete, and anytime you need extra labour around the farm, call on them. They will work for nothing more than meals, but they do eat a lot."

May nodded. "We will manage the meals, even after Imara and Kit return to school."

Imara reached down and took Henry's hand. She pulled him to his feet, and the tension was broken. The pack members introduced themselves to the Deegles, and everyone was neighbourly.

"So, Agent Noro, I am free to go?"

The elf glided over to her and inclined his head. "You are. Thank you for your cooperation. My partner will apologize to you at a later time; he has ego and pack standing to contend with."

"A brutal combination."

"Are you sure you will not join me for a meal, perhaps coffee?"

"No. I am good. Thanks though." She winked and scooped up Mr. E.

"This boyfriend of yours is a lucky man to have you so focused on him."

"Yeah, he's nearly as lucky as I am." She nodded to the assembled and headed for Bright Bell. There were stones to bury, and if the trees were on the way, the sooner she got the anchors set, the sooner Anderson would have his lands to roam again.

With unlimited labour on a guilt trip, there was no time left to lose.

Chapter Ten

Kitty was still gasping and giggling about the morning's events. "I can't believe it. You faced down an entire wolf pack."

"Exams are worse. This was just a standard neighbour dispute. The new guys were trying to see how far they could push. If not for your invitation, your family would have dealt with it, I am sure."

"Not as quickly and someone might have gotten hurt."

Imara smiled and patted the soil over the last stone. With the barrier in place, she powered it up. It was enough to last Anderson a few years of free wandering and a light top up could be done remotely.

"No one was hurt. I am a little scuffed up, and Mr. E has confiscated my favourite nightgown, so a few losses on my side, but nothing I can't survive."

Kitty got on her horse and waited with Bright Bell. When Imara was back in the saddle, they headed back to the farm with their hands covered in soil and sweat on their backs.

"So, was Agent Noro really flirting with you?"

Imara chuckled. "The fey don't flirt. For a nearly ageless species, they are shockingly direct. If they want you, they let you know."

"You said no?"

"I did. He isn't my type, and the lithe body type isn't my preference. I like a guy who looks like he can rescue you from danger and you get that feeling in the first glance." She smiled softly.

"Your face is doing that thing again. I can hardly wait to meet your guy."

Imara laughed. "Fine. I will ask him to go out for dinner or lunch with us on his day off."

They were back at the farmstead in a few minutes, and Kitty asked one more question, "So, is he really an XIA agent?"

"Yeah. We met in class."

"That is so cool. Back in a few minutes. These guys have gotten quite a workout today."

Imara headed to the hosepipe outside the barn, and she scrubbed her hands before pressing the wet skin to the back of her neck.

"You were working on something." The older male from the pack was next to her, and she left the stand and the barrel that caught the over pours.

"I was. Just wrapping up one project before the trees get here."

"They just arrived. The ladies are arranging lunch, and when the boys have earned it, they will eat."

"Great. With cooperation, we should be done in two hours. It's a good thing that your guys can dig."

He paused and blinked. "You mean the wolves?"

"Yup. They transgressed, so they need to make themselves useful. At each tree, we need a hole and then the tree planted and filled in."

"Do you know how many trees were ordered?"

Imara smiled, "Enough for our purposes. The sooner we start, the sooner we finish. Don't worry; the soil is soft. I have already dug the initial holes, and the trees go in to the left or right. If I can do it with my pathetic human hands, you wolves should be able to manage it."

His skin darkened with embarrassment. "Ah, right."

She laughed and walked over to the

driveway where the process of unloading was happening.

The quantity of trees was staggering, but then, the same quantity of rocks took a lot less space.

Andy asked her, "Can you explain what we are doing with these?"

Imara stood up on a bench, and she clapped her hands. "Right. Ladies and gentlemen. We are working to plant a security ring around the property. The beasts will be repelled by it, and the humans will be reminded of the barrier."

She made eye contact with everyone for a moment, keeping her gaze calm. "This morning, Kitty and I went around and buried stones with a power signature. The only person that they matter to lives on this property. Taking or removing them from their resting places will not benefit anyone unless you want a spectre in your room."

Henry raised his hand. "What is a

spectre?"

"A physical manifestation of a deceased mage, containing his power and intellect."

Anderson stepped forward. "I am a spectre."

Anna smiled at him, her mind appearing to have righted itself overnight. "He really is. He died twenty years ago, and here he stands today."

The wolves still didn't seem to understand.

Imara looked to Anderson, "May I?"

He nodded.

With a slight alteration of her energy flow, he went from solid to transparent. With a few steps, he walked to the young wolf and passed his hand through him.

When he stepped back, she powered him up.

He extended his hand to the young man, and they shook on it.

"Holy shit. How did you do that?"

Imara sighed and pinched the bridge of her nose. "I am a Death Keeper. It is what I do. It comes as easy to me as the fur form does to you. Now, who is ready to plant some trees?"

Kitty raised her hand. "I am!"

May nodded, "A few of us will stay here and prepare lunch. You have fun."

Imara looked around and found her shovel. "Oh, we will."

A quad was rigged with a trailer and delivered the trees to the sites. All Imara and the others had to do was trail after and dig holes.

The rush of binding the tree to the stone was powerful. She hadn't done it in ages, but she wanted to do more. It was the strange mix of life and death that made it so heady.

They had completed the first thirty trees when she heard the quad approaching again. A glance over her shoulder made her freeze in place. She stood with her hands grimy and everything else coated in sweat.

The rider dismounted and walked over to her, tipping up her chin for a kiss. "Hiya, Imara. I thought you could use a hand."

She went up on her toes without touching him with her grubby hands. When the kiss was over, she sank slowly to her heels. "Afternoon, Argus. You have a day off?"

"I was called because of a rogue Master Death Keeper threatening a young pack. I was on the road when you were texting me and laughing my ass off at the reports that Noro was filing."

She wrinkled her nose. "Did he call my judgment into question?"

"He definitely did. Apparently, you rebuffed his phenomenal attractiveness. That was according to him, not in the official file."

She blushed. "Right. Good. Well, not good but yeesh. He was persistent."

Argus pressed his forehead to hers. "You were unreasonably attached to your chosen mate. It baffled him. I, however, had a very different reaction."

"I am guessing you did, and as much fun as this is, not only are we not getting closer to lunch, but we are also the focus of many curious gazes."

He chuckled and straightened. "Right. What do you want me to do?"

"Dig holes next to the small holes I made earlier, put in a tree and go to the next one."

She flinched when his uniform shirt came sailing her way, and she tried not to look like she was looking as his footwear, socks and then pants and underwear were left on the quad.

His shift into his gryphon was like watching liquid gold filling a mold. He flew to the next site, and with two claw swipes, he had made a deep hole in the rich soil. Imara got on the quad and followed him with the pack scampering after.

As they filled the fifth hole that Argus had created, Henry looked at her with a grin. "So, that is your boyfriend?"

She blushed and kept working. "Yes."

"You don't share his scent."

"We are waiting until I finish school. I need to focus to get my degree, and after that, we have all the time we need. He's a slow-aging shifter, and my family lives into their nineties."

"You have planned this out."

"Of course. I have one life, and I don't want to waste it. My teen years were skewed because of circumstances beyond my control, but now that I am all grown up, I can pick and choose what I become and what I do."

Henry glanced at the figure of the gryphon flying above the trees, seeking the next sight. "He's what you want to do with your life."

"Part of it." She grinned and looked back at Henry. "The fun part of it."

He laughed, and they trudged off to the next gouged site. It wasn't a bad way to spend the morning.

Chapter Eleven

She was sitting with her hip pressed to Argus's when her phone went off. Imara rose from the bench and wandered off for some quiet. The occasional howl that broke from the pack was making everyone laugh.

"Hello?"

"Hello, Apprentice Death Keeper Mirrin? This is Mage Guide Leader Severance. I am just calling to confirm the visit to the spectral event for Monday night."

Imara blinked. "Of course. If you send me the list of names, I will make sure that the relatives of the girls are aware and ready for our visit."

"That will be wonderful. Thank you so much."

"I will meet you at the rest site. See you on Monday at seven in the evening. I will explain what Death Keepers do, and then, we will all go into the site. Those who are scared can hang back, but if any of the parents wish to come along, I am willing to work with their family spectres."

"That is amazing. We will see you there."

Imara hung up and sighed. Before she could forget, she put the information in her phone. "Damn, almost forgot about that."

Once she had secured the appointment, she returned to the table and snagged a passing slice of pie.

"You look like you saw a ghost, and for you, that is saying something." Argus murmured it in her ear.

"I was just reminded that I am volunteering with the Mage Guides on Monday night."

His shoulders started shaking. "You are going through with it?"

"I am. The more folks learn about Death Keepers, the more it will be a developing branch of study. It is the fear of death that stops folk from using the wisdom of passed mages."

Argus grinned. "You are practicing right now."

"Hell yes, I have to face nine Mage Guides on Monday night. It is a miracle I am not drinking." She stabbed the pie savagely.

Down the table, Mr. E was eating the pie that had been made for him alone, and the pack was cheering him on.

"Is he really eating an entire pie?"

Imara grabbed a second slice and got munching. "Yup. I have no idea where he gets it from."

Argus laughed again.

Imara looked around and kept eating until there was nothing more than crumbs left in the pie plate in front of her. She never could resist pie.

After the sun started to sink, Andy got up and thanked them all for helping them plant. The regular farm hands agreed that the help had been welcome, since they didn't have to do anything.

Imara joined the others in cheering and applauding their host's generosity. She did it lightly because her hands were raw from the digging.

"I hope this can become a fast friendship between our two properties. It was a bumpy start, but the Deegles stand ready to help with all of your seer needs. Oh, and dairy and wool."

The pack applauded and let out yips of agreement.

Kitty came over to Imara. "You get separate thanks later. Tomorrow, my dad is firing up the glass works, and you are going to get some custom pieces."

Imara smiled and yawned. "Sorry to be a party pooper, but I think I am going to have to turn in. It has been a tiring day."

"No worries. We will see you in the morning."

Imara turned to Argus. "I am sorry you came all this way, but I am beat."

"I loved helping out. Should you get calls for brute labour more often, I would love to find a way to be there." He wrapped his arm around her shoulder and gave her a hug.

"You used your other form."

He shrugged. "I was making a point. You have to with some of the new packs. It is a matter of strength."

"And you got to play in the dirt."

Argus snickered, "That too."

She groaned and flexed her hands, glancing over the crowd. "When did Noro and his guys get here?"

"While we were planting. It isn't often that we get to take part in rather enjoyable community activity."

"Do you know them?"

He chuckled. "Yeah, we train together on an annual basis. The wolf is a hot head, Noro is a tramp, and their undead member only moves when he has to. He should be pulling up in an hour or so."

"I don't think I am going to make it. I have to finish binding the trees, and then, I am going to be done for the night."

"What does that entail?"

She smiled softly. "Come with me."

Imara paused and checked in with Kitty, letting her know that she was turning in for the night.

"So soon? Grandpa was going to play his violin."

"I am sure I will be able to hear it. I am just a little tired, and I have one more task to do. I will see you in the morning."

Kitty nodded, but there was a frown between her brows.

Argus was waiting. She took him by the hand, leading him behind the house and to the spectre stone.

"What are you doing?"

"The most secret part of my job. Since you are law enforcement, I thought this would be educational for you." She breathed deeply and placed her hands on the stone.

* * * *

Argus watched as her body tensed. Light began to glow under her palms, and slowly, Imara took on the same glow.

Her breathing increased in speed, and the glow got brighter. When the light was blinding, she dug her fingertips into the stone, and the switch was flipped.

Light coursed out in a spoke pattern, streaking out to all edges of the property. As one, the trees lit up. All the new, small, wavy saplings thickened and became heavy and mature as the light burned within them.

She was aging the trees.

"Holy shit." He whispered it softly as the display continued. The family and pack gathered behind him to watch.

Slowly, the light faded, and she pulled what was left back into the stone. From the stone, it seeped back into her skin.

There was something about her posture that alerted him. He rushed forward and caught her as she fell.

Imara smiled. "There, now, he can last until all the trees are gone. If he wants to go earlier, they can just let me know."

Her lids were fluttering, and her pulse was beating fast in her neck.

"You need help."

She muttered softly. "I need sleep. If one freaking wolf scratches around my door tonight, I am going to use lightning."

"I will pass along the message." He lifted her higher and walked past the stunned audience.

Andy Deegle nodded. The Althos pack master nodded as well. No one was going to wake her up until she wanted to wake up.

Mr. E trotted along next to him, relaxed and casual. It made Argus feel considerably better. If her familiar wasn't worried, she was just tired.

The tiny house was ridiculously cute. Climbing the ladder to the sleeping loft wasn't easy, but once he had her in bed, he wasn't sure if he should help her out of her clothing.

May Deegle cleared her throat from the main floor. "I will take it from here, Agent."

He nodded. "Oh, thank you. That wasn't a conversation I wanted to have with her after the fact."

"I know. Shoo."

From the unconscious woman on the bed, he heard the distinct, "Night, Argus."

He grinned and headed down the ladder. "Good night, Imara. Good work today."

Her eyes opened slightly, she slowly raised one thumb before she closed her eyes and relaxed.

Argus left the tiny house, and May headed up the ladder to help Imara get ready for bed.

* * * *

May helped Imara out of her grimy clothing and shoes. "Imara, how can we repay you? Not only have you become one of Kitty's few friends, but you have also given consistently and selflessly. What can we do for you?"

Imara mumbled, "More pie, and do you know a tailor?"

May smiled at the young lady as she settled into bed. "What do you need a tailor for?"

"New robes. Upgrade and I got taller. They don't match anymore." She rubbed her nose in the quilt. "And quilts. I love the quilts."

May stroked the dark hair from her forehead. "I think that something can be done. You are a Master now?"

"Master Death Keeper. That's me." It was her last utterance; she fell back and was snoring gently in seconds.

May nodded and left the woman to her rest.

Once outside the tiny house, she grabbed Kitty and hauled her to the edge of the gathering. "Do you know her size?"

"Sure, me plus three inches and thirty pounds. She's a solid, tall size twelve."

"Excellent. Fire up the embroidery machine and get the patterns for Death Keepers from the internet. I need them coded as quickly as you can manage it."

"Why?"

"We are making her a present. I am heading into town and shaking up your aunty April."

May turned to her husband and let out a sharp whistle. The keys to the truck flew through the air in seconds. "Thanks, Honey."

She got into the car and headed into town. Having her mother-in-law restored to sanity and her father-in-law back to help work the farm was a gift that she had never imagined. The least she could do was use her family's fabric shop to outfit the Death Keeper appropriately. Anna could make the pie.

* * * *

Imara woke up feeling itchy. The sweat from the day before was fused on her skin. She could vaguely remember being tucked into bed, but now, she wanted a shower, a glass of water, and breakfast.

Her arms could barely hold her as she headed down the ladder. The shower helped, warming her muscles and getting rid of the dirt and sweat. She was nearly human when she left her small house with Mr. E pattering along beside her.

"Did you stay out long after I passed out?"

No, I curled up next to you, occasionally licking salt off your wrist. I am a cat after all.

She scooped him up and softly mashed his ears until he purred. "You are a kitten, and don't you forget it."

The scent of coffee was in the air, and

when she headed into the farmhouse, it was Anderson who was making it. Around the room, it looked as if a fabric bomb had gone off and taken the Deegles and the pack with them.

"They couldn't decide on a colour, so they made you one in brown, one in grey, and one in black." Anderson grinned.

"One what?"

"What did you ask for before you went to sleep?" He hinted.

"Pie?" It was a safe guess.

He chuckled. "I believe you are entitled to your Master's robes. That was what you mentioned to May, and she was the right person to talk to. My daughter-in-law is a champion seamstress who used to win every county fair with her needlework. She shifted to quilting after I died, but this was a chance she couldn't resist. That new machine of hers was chugging along all night."

Tears started to sting her eyes. "They made me robes?"

"Three different styles. Kitty got the patterns and made the sewing machine recognize them. Digitizing, I think they said. Everyone else was measuring, sewing, and checking the fit."

"How did they check the fit?"

"Anna noted that the pack alpha was the same size as you but one inch shorter. After that she was used for all pinning and assembly."

"Why is everyone lying around like the dead?"

"Well, it does take a contribution of living energy for the enchanting of the robes. With three sets of robes, everyone donated some energy. I don't know of many others who will be wearing power from seers, fey, shifters, and two undead."

She blushed. "The XIA donated as

well?"

"They have great community spirit, especially your fella. He only has eyes for you, you know."

She smiled. "I know. The feeling is mutual. Only two more terms and a license and I can do something about it."

Anderson raised his brows. "Marriage license?"

"No, business magic license. I am going to make my natural skill for the dead pay."

"Speaking of that, what did you do? I feel almost alive again."

She flexed her fingers and took the cup of coffee that he held out to her. "Ah, well, the saplings were given a taste of age. It was a division of power. I gave them some of you, and as you live here, your presence will be fed by their strong, vigorous lives. It is like a battery and a solar panel. They will charge you continuously, but you can also instantly appear at any point near a tree. If there is a disturbance, you can be there in a blink. If there is a lost lamb, missing calf, or a wild animal, you can be there in a heartbeat."

"What about Anna?"

She brushed the hair from her face and sighed, "I have primed the standing stone that you are embedded in. When she passes, either you can fade away, or I can set her in the stone as well. She can share the energy lines, and you two can exist here in any physical memory you have. You can both appear young again, or you can remain the doting grandparents."

"Speaking of which, what kind of woman is my granddaughter?"

Imara smiled. "She is a wonderful woman, good heart, strong magic, and willing to embrace whatever comes her way. She is the kind of woman to give you the shirt off her back in a blizzard and then pretend she isn't cold." She summed it up. "She is a very good friend."

"Good. She was a kind child, but I have not known her for twenty years."

"You know her now. Learn who she is now, and it is definitely a person worth knowing." She looked around. "Should I be here?"

He chuckled. "I was going to tend the animals and saw movement. Thought you could use the coffee."

"What time is it?"

"Five. Dawn was ten minutes ago."

"Oh, hell. I am going back to bed." She didn't know when Mr. E had made it to her shoulder, but she reached up to pet him. "Did you want to come along, or do you want to use our last hours here to chase sheep."

He was off her shoulder and at the door in seconds.

She opened the door, and the dark

streak disappeared. "I hope he doesn't hurt them or himself."

Anderson took her empty cup. "He won't. He's riding them."

The shock that ripped through her was followed by a bubbling laughter that wouldn't be contained. She sprinted out of the farmhouse, ran into the tiny house, and let the laughter loose.

When the mirth had faded, she checked the charge on her phone and tiptoed out of her small temporary home, heading for the sheep paddock. This was worthy of a photo.

Chapter Twelve

Kitty begged, "You have to send me a copy of that."

Mr. E let out a low growl.

"Um, I really don't think he wants me to share it. This image of the kitty riding along on the head of your ram will have to remain a myth or legend."

She stroked the embroidery of the grey Death Keeper robes.

Kitty glanced over without swerving. "Do you really like them?"

"I love them. They are gorgeous and far better than what I had in mind. I am humbled by the effort that your family and the pack put into it."

"I think we have been given adjunct

pack status. Now that everything is out in the open and a community has been forged, they are going to be nice and reliable neighbours." There was smug confidence in her tone.

"I still can't thank you enough for these robes. At least I will look somewhat official tomorrow night."

"I really want to see you give that talk to the Guides."

"You just got to witness the practice version. I am just wondering if I can make it plain-spoken enough to get it through to the kids."

"I am sure that you will be fine. What do you think Eckoak is going to have for us tomorrow?"

"With my luck, something involving precipitation." Imara grinned.

"Oh lord, not snow. I really hate snow." Kitty grumbled.

"Ladies, today we are working on

snow. You have to combine wind, cold air, water, and cloud density. When you make seven snowflakes, you can go."

Imara wrinkled her nose and looked at the black fabric on the ground around her. Kitty was across the practice area and on the same type of cover.

Imara smiled. "Last one to do it buys the burgers."

The challenge was on.

Rain, sleet, fog, they all came easy. Snow was more delicate.

Imara stood still and raised her hands as if lifting the cold air mass to the cloud cover she had managed. She pushed it up slowly, and the thick fog swirled. It moved in a slow twist, and soon, a single white object fluttered to the ground. Imara ignored it and kept going, using up the fog until the ground around her was covered with snow.

"Mirrin, you are dismissed. Go get some hot chocolate. I set up a carafe in the antechamber."

Imara was shivering and she nodded, heading off to the promise of hot sugar.

When she cupped the hot mug in her hands, she returned to the classroom and watched as Kitty found the move that worked for her. She used cold air into a rain cloud, but the result was the same.

One by one, small flakes separated from the cloud mass and drifted down to the black flooring.

"Good job, Deegle. Get your hot chocolate, and see you at the next class."

Kitty stumbled off the practice area, and Imara caught her, helping her out and to her own cup of hot chocolate.

"How long were we working on that?"

"Four hours?"

"Damn. That was intense. Do you wonder what our marks are?"

"Nope. This is pass or fail. Anything else is just annoying." Imara waited until they had both finished their beverages before she got her bag and Mr. E.

"Come on, Kitty, you are buying lunch."

"Yes, ma'am." Kitty laughed as they headed up on the lift.

Out in the sun, Kitty asked a question that she had obviously been mulling over. "So, you really aren't sleeping with Argus?"

"No, I am really not. We agree that he is mine and I am his, but no shenanigans of that nature until after I have my commercial magic license."

"Why wait? Why not just jump him after school is done?"

"Because of the contamination testing."

Kitty looked blank. "What?"

"If they feel you have been compromised by someone who isn't a mage, they can deny your license. It doesn't matter if he or she isn't an influence on you, they still can show up as a contamination of your magic. Having a lover from the extra-natural population who isn't a mage is enough of a factor to deny the initial license. After that, it doesn't matter."

Kitty blinked. "I didn't know that."

"They don't advertise it, but the Death Keepers have a lot of notes regarding membership in the Mage Guild. If you want, I can show you some of the early documentation. Reegar has it in his library."

"That would be wonderful. I confess that I saw those tomes and I started drooling."

Imara laughed. "It happens to us all."

They headed off and had their lunch, with Kitty only mentioning dealing with the Mage Guides twice.

The day was definitely not over.

Imara came out of the change room at

the spectre repository, and she was wearing her new Master's robes. The charcoal-coloured fabric was embroidered with dark pewter designs that denoted her rank and her occupation.

Master Wylkinson was manning the desk, and he whistled softly when she emerged with Mr. E on her shoulder. "Those are some great robes."

"Thank you. They were a gift from a friend." She turned and looked toward the door. Lights were beginning to enter the parking lot, and there were quite a few more than she was expecting.

"Are you all right to handle the crowd?"

"I am. Do you have a map of whom I can disturb?"

"All the alert spectres are eager to have visitors. Those who are not alert are indifferent." He shrugged, paused, and cleared his throat. "May I watch?"

"Oh, of course. I am just going to go

out and greet the troupe."

"Wait a moment until their Guild Master has them under control. Once they are attentive and focused, make your entrance."

She took one of the staffs with the lamp, and she waited in the shadows of the doorway. When the Guide Master had gathered forty people, Imara verified that her watch was correct, and she stepped out with her hood up.

The crowd stirred nervously when she approached, but when she lifted her chin and smiled in the friendliest manner she could manage, a few of the parents exhaled in relief.

"Guide Master, allow me to introduce myself. I am Master Death Keeper, Imara Mirrin. The local Death Keeper, Master Wylkinson, has allowed me to take you on an exploration of his grounds, and we will be able to meet a few of your ancestors in the process."

She looked to the serious little girls in front, all wearing their little uniforms with the blaze of fire on their shoulder. "Guides, how many of you are a little nervous about being here tonight?"

A few small hands went up.

"Good. Being honest is important. Now, who knows what a spectre is?"

One girl shot her hand into the air and answered before Imara could call on her. "They are the souls of dead mages."

"That is a common thought. What spectres are is an imprint of the magic left behind when there is no mage to control it. I will give you an example. Guides, who among you have a computer with photos on it?"

Eight of the nine girls raised their hands.

"Well, what happens if your computer breaks down? What happens to the files?"

One of the girls raised her hand.

"Yes?"

"My brother knocked a soda into the family computer, and we had to send it away to be fixed, but the information was gone. We got the pictures back, though."

Imara smiled. "Excellent example. In this case, the mage's body is the computer. It holds all the memory of everything it has ever done. When it was broken, the memory was gone, but the cloud and other information storage sites were able to help you put the data back together. Right?"

The little girl nodded.

"That is what a spectre is. It isn't the original; it is a log of all the information and experiences. It can't make a new opinion, and it can't change personalities. It is just a copy of the old information." She nodded toward the stones in the distance. "They are not scary; they are the information printed into magic.

No more, no less. Now, as for Death Keepers, what we do is we talk to the spectres, and using our magic, we can take those copies and let them inch into our current world. We can let strangers talk to them, let their families talk to them, and we wake them up so that they don't end when their soul has passed."

One of the girls had her hand up.

"Yes?"

"My grandpa died last year, and he is here. Can he talk to me?"

"Yes. If you want him to. That is another part of the job of the Death Keeper. If you don't want to talk to the spectre, we can make them stop."

The little girl nodded with wide eyes.

"Now, as part of the introduction to Death Keepers, I will explain the clothing."

She extended her arms. "As far back as mage records go, Death Keepers have worn the long robes in the repositories.

The spectres expect us to look like this, so it makes communication easier. You know that Guild Officers dress like Guild Officers, and bakers dress like bakers. You expect a uniform and you need to see it. As I have mentioned, spectres are not capable of learning on their own, this is one of the reasons for the uniform. Now, the staff and the lamp. That one is easy, can anyone guess?"

One of the girls shot her hand up. "You work in the dark?"

"That is correct. While you can address a spectre during the day, they are harder to see. The magic of the Death Keepers makes the spectres glow, and when they glow, we can see them. Night makes it easier to see them."

She looked to the adults, "Now, does anyone have any questions before we go for our little walk?"

One of the fathers looked at her with a grim expression. "Why are you called

Death Keepers if the spectres aren't souls?"

"Because the spectres are removed after death. They can't be pulled while someone is alive by the average Death Keeper. Also, in the old days, the distinction was as fuzzy as it is today. No one made a distinction between a ghost and a spectre. Ghosts are trapped souls; spectres are chatty magic exclusive to mages."

A woman blurted her question, "Why is it so expensive?"

Imara had been waiting for that question. "Since so few mages have themselves tested for death affinity, it is an in-demand occupation. The spell work required is taxing, and few Death Keepers can comfortably create a spectre or a holding stone. It is a draining process that needs more respect. Nocturnal vultures is a common epithet, but we show up night after night and let folks talk to loved ones, recover everything from family spells to favourite recipes. We keep the dead company and comfort the living. That is why it is so expensive; you are literally buying a portion of our lives." She smiled brightly. "Now, let's go on into the repository, and I will explain the security features."

Two hours of the gathered Guides and their families talking to the spectres and even the Guide Master tearing up as she spoke to her great-grandmother left Imara tired. Mr. E purred against her neck, and he kept her calm while she shook hands with all of the visitors and got a surprise hug from the Guide Master.

When the cars were gone, she turned back to Master Wylkinson. "Thank you for that. If we can manage one recruit out of that batch, I would be over the moon."

He was staring at her. "Do you want a job here? Seriously. You can have my job. Those spectres are more alive than they have been in decades."

She rubbed at her forehead and headed back to the office. "Nope. I have my own plan, and it doesn't involve working nights all the time."

"What is your plan?"

"Spectral consulting. I will gladly come here and supercharge your facility, but the guild will have to pay." She grimaced and put the lamp back in its holder.

Master Wylkinson paused for a moment, and then, he smiled. "When you open your office, send me your card. This is a service I would gladly charge folks extra for."

She laughed. "I will. Should be late next year if the Mage Guild grants me the license."

"I look forward to the card in the

mail, or if you want to bring more Mage Guides here, you can come anytime." He bowed.

She sighed. "You think I did okay?"

"I think that you made Death Keeping accessible and understandable. The spectres you bolstered were delighted for the added energy, and their families have made appointments to return in the next few days."

"Good. The effect should last anywhere from a week to a month."

"Thanks. I am sorry I was so rude on the phone."

She smiled and pulled her hood back. "No problem. We usually work with the dead, after all."

He laughed and extended his hand. "It is a situation I will change the moment you are available again."

Imara grinned and shook his hand. All in all, it was a good night for her reference page.

Chapter Thirteen

Smara blinked at the command, and then, she looked to see if Kitty had heard what she had.

"Don't just stand there, I want you to go topside and clear up the thunderstorm without affecting the surrounding area."

"Um, Professor Eckoak, that is a little beyond us."

"Really? You two have separately created weather systems; together, you should be able to take down a storm without wrecking the local weather system. Go on up and give it a shot."

"We can work together?" Kitty's eyes were hopeful.

"Of course. I don't want you to die. If you two can't manage it, you fail. Well, you will be given a barely passing grade, but you won't pass with flying colours. For that, I need a rainbow."

Imara looked to Kitty, and they headed to the lift. Mr. E sat up from his bath time and blinked. *You are leaving?*

"We are going to break up the storm up top. Are you coming?"

This I have got to see and possibly offer an opinion on.

Imara extended her hand, and he ran up her arm, settling on her shoulder. She grabbed her bag, and she and Kitty stood close on the lift.

Kitty lifted her hands and created a dry bubble around them. "This is going to be tricky."

"No kidding. First, we have to contain it and then—"

Do you need to contain it? Check the local weather.

Imara grabbed her phone and looked for the local information. "Holy shit."

"What?"

"Our instructor built this storm, just for us. The surrounding areas are clear and sunny. All we have to do is unravel this carefully, and it should fall apart."

Kitty exhaled slowly. "That is something. So, we just have to contain and dismantle weather magic. No problem."

"Right. So, sorry, but we need to get a feel for the temperature."

Mr. E hid in her hair as the wind lashed at them and the heat in the air was apparent.

Imara pulled a solid bubble of warm air around them. "Well, that was fun. Okay, so high humidity, low pressure, and minimal precipitation. If we use cold, we are going to have a tornado. So, thoughts?"

Kitty frowned and looked around. "I know you are going to hate me, but how about lightning? It will drain some of the pressure system and cause a cascading reaction through the cloud layer. I think tearing the sky a new one might be what we need."

"I am willing, but we are going to have to ground it far enough away from us that we won't get zapped."

"I can take the statue on the far side of the field; you can take the one outside that parking structure." Kitty bit her lip.

Imara looked around and saw her distant target. "Right, well, I am going to drop the bubble, are you ready?"

"Yup." Kitty flexed her fingers. "Up, from the bottom, right?"

"You got it. Mr. E, hold on." She dropped the air bubble.

The wind hit her, and she staggered. As soon as she could, she focused on calling heat down from the clouds while pushing energy up through the distant statue.

Lightning crackled in a jolt that made her jump. She pushed and did it again, and again, draining the clouds of the magic that powered them.

Behind her, she heard matching crackling and booming, and the sky began to show through. They kept it up, draining the sky of magic until a rainbow arched over the administration building.

Imara sat heavily on the grass, and she looked to see Kitty kneeling with a stunned expression on her face. "Did we do it?"

Eckoak appeared from the lift and looked at the sign of their efforts. "Took you long enough. You should have been able to drain it with four strikes, but well done, ladies. You pass. High marks. Ninety-three percent for the both of you."

The grumpy dryad left them, and they were stuck staring at each other.

Kitty started laughing, then Imara followed suit. They sat in the grass with the sun beaming down on them, revelling in the fact that they hadn't killed anyone.

* * * *

Mirrin Deepford looked out her office window and saw the rainbow. "Thank goodness."

Eckoak appeared in the chair next to the desk. "No kidding. I thought they were going to fry each other."

"And yet you let them try to break the sky, Koki."

Eckoak shrugged. "They needed to learn. They still think that it was magic in the sky and not natural energy. I believe that I will save that little informational tidbit for their post-class briefing."

"You didn't build that storm?"

"Nope. I had it blown in by another weather mage overnight. They managed to burst it and keep it from travelling, which is all I was after. You have a good kid there. Makes me almost wish I had reproduced myself."

Mirrin laughed. "That is a frightening thought. Where are the girls now?"

"The women are laughing their asses off in the meadow over the classroom. All that power has a somewhat euphoric effect. It's why most weather mages are so damned cheerful."

Mirrin looked to her friend and shrugged. "Glad you are in a good mood then."

Eckoak waved her hands. "Give me your computer; I need to enter in their marks, so I can get the hell out of Dodge."

"I thought you were writing a post-class report."

"I am coming back." Eckoak sighed in

exasperation. She grabbed the laptop, logged in, and her fingers flew in a rapid blur that was hard to watch.

Mirrin smiled and cocked her head. "Where did you learn to type?"

"It was a misspent youth. I still prefer the Dvorak keyboard, but this is fine." She typed for a few minutes, saved her work, and then logged out.

"There, Mirrin, you daughter's grades are final. You can breathe now."

"She succeeds or fails on her own. I am not using any clout to get her a passing grade."

Eckoak stood and stretched. "You don't have to, she's your daughter. Lucky too. It was like she could figure out everything and then used hand signals to pass the information on to Deegle."

"It isn't cheating."

"No, but it is a little weird. Ah, well, I will see you in a few weeks before you get all crazy with the next term."

Mirrin rubbed her neck and then smiled. "Thanks for teaching this course."

"You are welcome. It was fun to see what your genetics can do in a proper receptacle. She's impressive, and I get the feeling that she is destined for surprising things."

"She wants to open a consulting business."

"She will be good at it. If she teams up with the Deegle girl, she might even go further with it than she can imagine."

Mirrin sighed. "I don't think she imagines much. She wants stability and is willing to do what she can to achieve it. That is what the whirlwind of courses is all about."

"Whatever. I tried to be nice, and you disagreed with me. See you in a few weeks. Good day, Chancellor."

Mirrin stared at the spot where the

dryad had been, and she leaned back in her chair. "Further than she can imagine, huh? I am looking forward to seeing it."

* * * *

Bara was waiting when they got back. "So, how was your weather class?"

"Pretty good. I think we just had a surprise exam."

Bara frowned. "Really? I had a present for Mr. E. I think he would enjoy it."

Present?

"You can still give it to him."

Bara grinned and headed into the kitchen area. When she returned, she held out some tiny objects, and Mr. E wasted no time in putting on the tiny yellow galoshes and standing up on his hind feet. The bright miniscule umbrella set off his black fur.

Imara snuck her phone out and took another picture.

You have to stop doing that. It was hard to take him seriously as he pranced around like an itty-bitty bear in his little boots.

Imara tried to fight her laughter, she really did, but instead of fighting it, she created a miniscule raincloud above Mr. E's head, and he stomped around, completely dry.

When her giggles had faded, she dissipated the cloud and licked her fingers.

Bara stared at her. "Did you just make it rain indoors?"

"I think so. His boots look wet, so I am guessing I did."

"Wow. That's... wow. Is it complicated?"

"Is what complicated?" She burst into giggles again. "Damn, I think I am high on magic."

Reegar appeared and gave her a long

look. "Weather magic. Have you been using lightning?"

She nodded and went off into giggles as Mr. E tried to pull his little boots off.

"Magic, ozone, nitrogen, and oxygen. It will wear off in an hour or two. Just stay away from your kitten and you will be fine. Maybe follow your friend's example and sleep it off."

Imara sighed. "Boring! I am going to help Mr. E get his boots off, and then, I am going to braid his hair."

She lunged, and all hell broke loose.

"I am fine now. You can untie me." Imara sighed.

"Oh, no. I am not falling for that one again." Bara scowled and pulled her still sticky hair away from her face.

"Listen, I didn't know I could make it rain soda. I am sorry." She tried to put her sincerity into her voice. "I am very, very sorry, Bara."

She looked down at her feet, "You, too, Mr. E. I am really sorry."

His fur was all matted, and he was giving her a homicidal glare. *You are going to owe me for this.*

She didn't know what he meant until he moved behind her and the ropes were shredded. She flexed her wrists and got to her feet.

Bara was shocked. "Why did he let you go?"

Imara wrinkled her nose. "I stopped laughing at him. He knew it had worn off."

She ran the water until it was warm to the touch and got a clean cloth. She filled a basin with warm water and sat at the table. Mr. E came up to her, and he stepped into it.

Imara dipped the cloth in the water and squeezed it out, blotting the soda out of his fur an inch at a time.

"It is a good thing that you are this

size. It makes it easier to undo this."

Bara sat at the table. "I am next."

"I am not going to wash all of you."

Bara snorted, "I just don't want to touch any of my stuff on the way to the shower. You will pick up my clothing, hang up my towel, and close the door after me."

"Yes, ma'am." She continued to get the sticky residue out of her kitten for another ten minutes.

When he was dry and curled up in a clean, dry towel, she went to act as Bara's butler for a few minutes.

After she was finished cleaning up the floor from the impromptu soda storm, she sat in exhaustion and looked at Reegar. He was sitting near the library with a book in his hands. "So, power drunk?"

"Apparently. My instructor didn't mention it."

"Eckoak is not very forthcoming with mundane bits of information."

"You have that right." She leaned back and tried to relax tense muscles.

"What is your next insane course?" He raised his brows.

"Just a little bit of stealth magic. Nothing serious."

Reegar jumped to his feet and headed into the library. He came back to the table and dropped a stack of books three feet high on the wood. "Read these and then tell me it isn't serious. Can't you take another course?"

She frowned. "What do you mean? Stealth magic is just like enchanted hide and seek, right?"

"Start reading. If you still want to take the course after you finish them, I will help you all I can." He left her alone.

Not one to ignore assistance when it was offered, Imara started reading the stack of tomes, and by the third, there was a nauseated feeling in her brain.

By the fifth book, she was shaking.

Stealth magic wasn't quite what she thought it was when she chose it for its high credit load.

I will help as well. I was a master of most of the skills of assassination and concealment. It is how I was able to make it into the homes of so many demon-contaminated mages. His little nose and wide eyes peeped out of the towel, at odds with his subject matter. *The key to stealth magic is to calm your soul before beginning anything. You already have mastery of that move from your work with the spectres. If you wish to do it, I will help you through it.*

Reegar returned. "So? What do you think so far?"

"I am petrified, but I am going to do it. Mr. E says he has used the magic before, and I trust him."

Reegar heaved a sigh. "Well, in that case, read these."

He beckoned, and a stack of books

came floating toward the desk. "These are on practical exercises and means to strengthen the reflexes you will need. Your gentlemen caller will be able to help you with the physical assault aspects."

She wrinkled her nose. "Is that really necessary?"

"It is if you want to come out of the course whole in mind and body. How did you even get in?" He growled it.

"I had a recommendation from my domestic magic instructor. She said I had a natural talent for assassination. I thought she was being funny."

Reegar closed his eyes and covered them with his hands. Imara got the feeling that if he wasn't already dead, he would have wished it on himself. When he sat up, he took a deep breath to steady his nerves, and he looked at her. "Right, the first thing you need to know is the art of being still."

She smiled and focused. After an hour of lectures, she came to one important discovery, if she acted like Mr. E, everything would become easy. It was as terrifying as it was encouraging, and she tried to find a middle ground.

Two more terms and she would be out on her own. What was she going to do without Reegar and Bara?

Kitty groaned and clutched her head on the sofa. "What happened?"

"You got caught in a storm. Go back to sleep." Imara grinned and fished out her phone to order pizza. She had just gotten through one of the toughest courses at Depford College, her friends were with her, and one of the toughest courses at the college was looming. She really needed a celebration.

You had to celebrate the small stuff, or the big stuff could pull you under.

Author's Note

Apologies for the delay, I have had a few medical issues between April and October. Getting back on track will be difficult, but I aim to give it a whirl.

I hope I have put in enough teasers for book four, *Stealth Magic 401*, but if not, be assured that Imara will run into more of her brothers (as soon as I find the list where I gave all their names and characteristics), and she might even meet her dad.

It could happen. Totally.

Thanks for reading,

Viola Grace

About the Author

Viola Grace (aka Zenina Masters) is a Canadian sci-fi/paranormal romance writer with ambitions to keep writing for the rest of her life. She specializes in short stories because the thrill of discovery, of all those firsts, is what keeps her writing.

An artist who enjoys a story that catches you up, whirls you around and sets you down with a smile on your face is all she endeavours to be. She prefers to leave the drama to those who are better suited to it; she always goes for the cheap laugh.

She is also the proud guardian of the

real Mr. E who has grown to two-armful proportions (and his slightly smaller stripey brother, Tsumugi). Twenty percent of all profits generated by the Hellkitten Chronicles goes to the support of his favourite charity, the Winnipeg Pet Rescue Shelter, who helped his brother and sister find a forever home... together.